Misty Mornings

Blueberry Beach Novels, Volume 5

Jessie Gussman

Published by Jessie Gussman, 2021.

MISTY MORNINGS

First edition. July 20, 2021.

Written by Jessie Gussman.

Cover art by Julia Gussman
Editing by Heather Hayden[1]
Narration by Jay Dyess[2]

~~~

Click HERE[3] if you'd like to subscribe to my newsletter and find out why people say "Jessie's is the only newsletter I open and read."

~~~

1.   https://hhaydeneditor.com/

2.   https://www.facebook.com/SayWithJay

3. https://BookHip.com/FASFD

Chapter 1

Graduation night, Blueberry Beach High, eighteen years ago

Leiklyn Weaver, brand-new high school graduate, sat on the knoll by the shore of Lake Michigan, the looming specter of Indigo Inn at Blueberry Beach behind her, with her two best friends in the world on either side of her, staring off into the darkness of the water.

Growing up in Blueberry Beach, there had been plenty of times she had been on the beach at three AM.

This could well be one of the last.

Maybe the beginning of the end.

Commencement meant beginning. She couldn't help but feel that it was an end as well.

Typical thoughts for a recent high school grad, probably.

On her right, Tiffany, a cheerleader and president of the science club, sighed. "I think we're supposed to be happy today. But I've been fighting a weird sadness."

Leiklyn jerked her head to the side. Her friend had been sad? She hadn't had any idea. Tiffany was one of those people who were always bubbly and happy and never met a stranger.

Before Leiklyn could say anything, Willan, who sat on Leiklyn's left, said, "Me too. I mean, graduation was great, and I had fun partying tonight, but there's almost a desperation, like nothing will ever be the same again."

Maybe that's why Tiffany and Willan were Leiklyn's best friends. They'd all felt the same thing, even though none of them had talked about it until just now.

"I did something yesterday. Something crazy," Leiklyn said, not because she wanted to change the subject, not even really because she wanted to cheer them up. Just because she didn't like to be sad. Who did?

Lord knew she had enough bad stuff in her short history that she could end up being sad and depressed for the rest of her life, and she was only eighteen years old.

Hopefully, the next eighteen years produced better memories, not the wretched ones that caused nightmares that would grab her out of a sound sleep, cover her in cold sweats, and give her a deathly fear of hell because she'd done something so terrible God could never forgive her.

Shaking those thoughts away quickly, or they would pull her down, she wiggled her shoulders, bumping both of her friends and giving them an excited grin which they could see easily under the three-quarters moon in the clear night sky.

"You finally said yes when Jake asked you out?" Tiffany guessed immediately.

"No," Leiklyn said, trying to keep the excitement in her voice. She hadn't been interested in dating. Not for three years. Not since Ethan and she...

No more thinking about the bad stuff.

"Guess again," Leiklyn encouraged them.

"You applied for the internship in Amsterdam. The one you've been talking about all year."

"Well, actually I did do that. A week ago, but we were so busy with finals and graduation and all those other things, I guess I forgot to tell you."

"We're your best friends, and you forgot to tell us?" Willan asked incredulously.

"I'm sorry," Leiklyn said immediately, knowing how Willan felt about their friendship. They told each other everything, and when Willan said everything, she meant *everything*.

She was very particular, dotting all of her I's and crossing all of her T's, and expecting everyone else to do it too. Everyone had their faults, and Leiklyn loved Willan even if Leiklyn's more casual approach to life annoyed Willan.

Sometimes, she wished she had been more stringent.

"It's okay. I guess we were busy. I fell off the wagon on my diet again." Willan pushed her feet out, her hands on the thighs which she claimed were too large.

Willan was a size ten, and she thought she was too big. No matter what Leiklyn and Tiffany told her, she dieted constantly, always with the goal of being model thin.

She hadn't dated any in high school because she couldn't believe that anyone would actually like her since she considered herself to be "fat."

"I'll start with you again tomorrow if you want me to," Leiklyn offered, although dieting was the last thing she needed to do. She'd been blessed with the kind of genes where she could eat anything and never gain an ounce. She actually had to lie about her weight in order to give blood, not meeting the requisite one hundred ten pounds. That was one thing she hadn't shared with Willan, because she knew it would discourage her.

"Did you decide to move out of your house?" Tiffany asked, knowing Leiklyn had been thinking about it for a while. Ever since her mom had gotten remarried and brought in three new stepsiblings, who seemed to take up all of her time. Not to mention her mom was talking about moving away from Blueberry Beach and down to Chicago where her stepdad's family was from.

All she seemed to want from Leiklyn anymore was to babysit her stepsiblings, and while Leiklyn didn't mind doing it some, she resented feeling like slave labor as she watched them every night after school and every Saturday evening so that her mom and her stepdad could have a date night.

She supposed it shouldn't upset her, since she wasn't interested in having a date night.

"You decided to start dating again," Willan said, almost sounding like she hoped that *wasn't* what Leiklyn had decided.

"I've done that too, but I'm going to wait until I go to college. And then I'm going to say yes to every boy that asks me."

"Even if you don't really like him?" Tiffany asked, a little incredulously.

"Yep. I'm going to date everyone. The only word coming out of my mouth in college will be 'yes.'"

"See? That's what happens when you go on too stringent a diet. Whether it's food or whether it's boys. You fall off, and you end up gorging yourself." Willan knew what she was talking about, since she'd pretty much done every diet known to man since junior high.

"You don't date, either," Leiklyn said, stating the obvious.

"That's because I'm too fat for anyone to like me. When I lose these flabby thighs and get my stomach tightened up so that there's not a big ripple in it, then I'll date. Although not everyone. I'm only going to date that one special boy—my soulmate. I'll know him when I see him."

Leiklyn said that last line with Willan in her own head. Willan said it so many times Leiklyn knew exactly what she was going to say.

That was one thing about having good friends and knowing them all your life. You could finish their sentences.

"I give up," Tiffany said, and that was typical, too. Everything came easily to Tiffany, and when something didn't, she had a tendency to walk away rather than digging in and trying hard.

Leiklyn probably had the opposite problem. Nothing came easily to her, not finances, not social situations, and especially not her family, which'd been busted up when she was little, and she'd been involved in shifting family dynamics all of her life as her mom hooked up with one man after another and broke up or divorced, and her dad's presence was sporadic.

Leiklyn loved games, guessing games, card games, even hide-and-seek and flashlight tag. Those were the best things about watching her new stepsiblings. They enjoyed playing with her, and she really did love watching them.

The problem was the attitude of her mom and stepdad, who expected her to be their built-in babysitter. All the time.

"I bought Indigo Inn," she said, jerking her head to the large, looming shadow behind her, sure her friends could feel the shiver of excitement that went through her as close as they were sitting together.

"You bought it?" Tiffany said, disbelief in her tone. Tiffany came from the perfect family. Her parents were still married, and they had plenty of money.

She had no idea what it was like to live like Leiklyn had. The unstable family, the constant struggle over money, never knowing whether she was going to have a new dad or not, and when she did, her mom expected her to act like he meant something to her even though she really didn't give a flip. What was the point when he was just going to leave?

"That's what I said," she said, enjoying her friends' disbelief.

"There has to be a catch. Kids don't buy houses. And this one's not even for sale," Willan, logical as always, injected into their conversation.

"So there's a catch?" Tiffany asked.

"Not really," Leiklyn said, stretching her legs out in front of her, putting her arms around both of her friends, and pulling them close. "The township took possession of it because of unpaid fines from the grounds being unkempt. They don't do it too often, but normally, they sell these things to anyone who will pay the balance of the fines. But my stepdad's brother has a friend who's a county commissioner, and I happened to be sitting with him at the wedding reception, and I don't really ly even remember how we got on the subject, but we talked, he pulled a few strings and talked to a couple of people, and I was able to purchase the house for a dollar."

"But you're a kid?!" Willan said.

"I'm eighteen. And I had a dollar, and I promised to mow the grass and make sure someone took care of the upkeep. I think they just wanted ed it off their hands because tourist season is coming up, and you know they'll be busy with other things."

Her friends were quiet for a bit, although they both leaned into her. They might not always agree on everything, and sometimes, they had the normal push and pull along with a little bit of envy and the struggle that friends have to get through to get along and accept each other's faults.

But they'd been friends since kindergarten. Even before that, actually, since they'd gone to the same church and knew each other before they even went to school.

It was hard to break bonds like that. None of them had any desire to.

"That's brilliant," Tiffany said, and she didn't sound the slightest bit jealous or upset. In fact, she sounded impressed. "I would never have thought of buying a house."

"It's not a house. It used to be a hotel. It's called Indigo Inn at Blueberry Beach, and there must be something like twenty bedrooms in it. Plus a ballroom. Plus...all kinds of stuff, I've heard." Willan knew everything about everything, and if anyone would know what was inside the house, she would.

"I haven't been in it yet, because I do have to cough up the money for the closing, to pay the lawyers and all those fees for the title transfers and, I don't know, whatever happens when someone buys a house. It's set for next month, and I need to come up with almost two thousand dollars."

"I have one thousand dollars in my savings account. I was going to use it to travel around a little bit the week before I go to college, but...if you let me in on the house, I'll give you the money." Tiffany ran a hand down her long leg as though making sure there was no sand stuck to her skin.

Leiklyn didn't have to think about that very long. Why wouldn't she want her best friend on the deed with her? "You're in."

"I just have a couple hundred dollars. I was saving so I could buy all the things I need to start the air fryer diet plan, but if you let me in, I'll give it to you. And I'll see if I can get some more."

"That's enough. It's not really about how much we give, it's about giving what we can," Leiklyn said, not wanting Willan to feel bad because Tiffany had more money than either one of them. It irritated her sometimes, but Tiffany was never unkind about it. "I think between the three of us, we can come up with enough to cover the rest. But the problem that I'm having is...who's going to take care of it while we're gone?"

Chapter 2

Leiklyn sighed and adjusted her hands on her friends' shoulders.

All three of them were going away to college. And none of them would be in Blueberry Beach come September. Winter came early in this northern part of the United States, but the grass would still need to be mowed and little repairs made so the township didn't feel the need to fine the inn again.

"That's a problem, it's also going to be an issue during the winter...what in the world are you going to do with it?" Tiffany stumbled a little then blurted out.

"Well, you probably don't have to heat the whole thing, like, there are probably different zones or whatever, so it could be a house."

"That's a big house. How would your kids feel about growing up in something they could get lost in?"

Leiklyn swallowed. They were touching a little too close to her deepest, darkest secret that not even Tiffany and Willan knew. "I don't know. Maybe someday we'll make it into a bed-and-breakfast. That would be cool."

"Leiklyn," Willan said, turning her head as though trying to study her friend in the moonlight.

"What?" Leiklyn asked, hearing that note in Willan's voice that said she'd just figured something out.

"You know my dad's friend, Ethan Fields's dad, lost his job and has been living with us for the last six months. My mom hates him. She says he's like Dad's identical twin brother and it is all she can stand to live with my dad. She doesn't want to live with his twin too. She's making him leave."

"Yeah?" Leiklyn said, wondering if Willan was going where she thought she was going with that.

"He could live there."

Yep. That's exactly what she was thinking. She wasn't sure how she felt about that, considering the history that she and Ethan had.

She hadn't managed to completely avoid him over the last three years, but she had managed to completely keep from talking to him.

Willan put her hand up. "I know. I know how you feel about Ethan. Even though I don't know why, and you refuse to say why you hate him, it would just be Mr. Fields. I heard them talking last night, and Ethan joined some group. It's like the Peace Corps, only different, and he's going to Central America to work on some kind of humanitarian missionary mission or whatever. I wasn't really paying attention, but he's not going to be here. I think they said he was leaving in the middle of this month. He'll definitely be gone by the time it closes."

"Wasn't Mr. Fields a carpenter?" Tiffany asked, scrunching up her brows and shifting a little. It was always hard for her to sit still.

"He was. That's what made me think of it. I don't know why Mom doesn't like him. He's always fixing things around the house. He fixed the hinge on my door and the latch on the window in my bedroom. He cleaned out the flowerbeds and got rid of all the weeds and junk that Mom had let go. He planted stuff that looks really good. I bet he probably couldn't pay you rent or anything, but if you just need someone to stay there and take care of things, I bet he'd do it."

If Ethan wasn't going to be there, Mr. Fields was the perfect choice.

Everyone always tried to avoid Willan's house because her mom was always in a bad mood and complained about everything. She'd even yell at them even if she wasn't in a particularly bad mood. As bad as Leiklyn's own home was, she preferred it over Willan's.

Stepsiblings and all.

"Are you ever going to tell us why you hate Ethan?" Tiffany asked. "After all, we'll be heading our separate ways, and we might never see each other again."

"I can't believe you've kept whatever it is from your best friends. And for years."

"Sometimes, things end badly," Leiklyn said, the same thing she'd said for years. Ever since Ethan and she...broke up.

"But it's been three years. I don't understand why you refuse to even look at him."

Leiklyn took a breath and blew it out before dropping her arms, pulling her legs up, and wrapping her arms around them. Tucking her body in close and tight. Mostly for protection, even if it was emotional protection.

"Maybe if I get away from here for a bit, things will clear up, and I'll be able to stand looking at him in, oh, I don't know, twenty years or so," she said, listening to the gentle lap of the lake along the shore. The lake was quiet and peaceful tonight, unlike the swirling, hot anger. Guilt. There was a lot of hot, heavy, raging guilt in her chest.

Why would she have bought Indigo Inn right here in Blueberry Beach when she couldn't wait to get away? Couldn't wait to see if new scenery would ease this ache in her chest and in her heart. If it would somehow assuage the guilt that gnawed at the insides of her ribs constantly.

Her friends let it go. No matter the begging and the pleading and the cajoling and the threatening they'd done over the years, she'd never been willing to say.

Saying the words out loud made them even worse than when they were quiet and hidden away secretly in her heart.

No one could ever find out what she had done. Ethan was the only one who knew, although he had blood on his hands too, and that was what had come between them.

It had opened up a chasm that, even though she and Ethan had grown up together and had been best friends, they couldn't get past. It was too big.

As far as she knew, Ethan felt the same way about her as she did about him. And rightfully so. She deserved his hatred.

"So once Ethan leaves," Leiklyn began, "We can ask Mr. Fields if he'd be interested in staying at Indigo Inn."

"Do you want us all to go to ask him?"

"If all of us are going to be on the deed, we all need to help get things taken care of." Leiklyn tilted her head. That might be too much. "But we'll just all pitch in where we can, all right? No rules, just everyone do what they can, the way we've always done things."

"Do you really think we're not going to see each other again?" Tiffany asked, her usual buoyant personality slipping back into the melancholy that had haunted them all during this day that was supposed to have been cheerful and exciting.

"We might think that we're different, but how many people who graduated last year do you see around town?" Willan asked, sounding reasonable again. Sometimes, her reasonableness, her attention to details, and her intellectual knowledge were uncannily accurate and astute.

"That's true. Even the ones who didn't go to college went to Chicago to get jobs." Tiffany tucked her own legs up and put her chin on her knees, staring at the rippling waters of the lake.

"That's not going to happen to us." Leiklyn wanted to reassure them, but her words came out more like a question.

"Everyone always says they're gonna be different, but they never are. You just lose track of your high school friends. Especially since we're not going to college together."

"I couldn't get in. I'd be going to college with you guys if either one of your schools would have accepted me. They just didn't." Tiffany's words were flippant, but there was still a sharp edge of sadness in them that Leiklyn had no trouble recognizing. It made her own heart squeeze. Tiffany was popular and fun and had a solid family and lots of money, but she'd struggled with the academics that came so easily to Willan and Leiklyn.

"If we own this house together, we'll have to see each other," Leiklyn said finally.

"Lots of people have parents and siblings and all kinds of family members here, and they never come back. There just isn't anything here," Willan said.

Her tendency to be negative was discouraging, and Leiklyn supposed they were good at balancing each other out, because while Willan had a tendency to keep her feet on the ground and to take their ideas and make sense of them, Leiklyn was usually able to take Willan's negative attitude and turn it into something positive.

She did this now. "Fine. Maybe we will lose track of each other. Maybe we'll go our separate ways and never see each other again, but we can make a decision today not to let that happen."

"Like everyone else, but it never works out the way you think."

"Let's make a pact." Leiklyn stood up, the long skirt she had worn to this evening's party blowing in the Lake Michigan breeze. "We'll do it right now. Come on, get up," she encouraged when her friends just looked at her.

"What kind of pact?" Tiffany asked, sounding a little grumpy as she stood, every inch of her long, toned legs exposed by the short shorts she wore.

"A pact so we won't live the rest of our lives without ever seeing each other again."

"It's not going to mean anything. People never keep those either," Willan said, standing and tugging down on her T-shirt, then brushing the sand off her jeans.

"We will. We will make a pact that we will come back to Blueberry Beach, and we'll meet on the porch of Indigo Inn, remembering that we purchased it together..."

When? When could they do it? A year didn't seem like long enough, but twenty years or thirty? They could be dead by then. They'd be old anyway. Their lives would pretty much be over.

"In eighteen years," Tiffany said. "That means we're halfway there right now. We'll do another eighteen years, and if we don't see each other again, we'll make sure that we meet on the porch of the inn."

"What day?" Willan asked, getting the details right as always.

Man, Leiklyn was really going to miss her friends. Sometimes, she wanted to grow up so bad she could taste it, and other times, she wanted to be a little girl again. Not have to go through all these hard things, like thinking about leaving her friends and thinking about why she hated Ethan so much.

"Today. It's June 1. We'll meet on June 1." Tiffany grinned at the two of them, her naturally exuberant personality coming out.

"There's nothing special about June 1. And technically, it's 3 o'clock in the morning on June 2," Willan said.

"True." Tiffany shoved her hands in her shorts' back pockets and looked down at the sand.

Leiklyn was sure Willan's brain was running over the problem, going to come up with a solution that would work for everyone.

"We could meet on Christmas?" Tiffany suggested.

"We might have families. We might be living in different parts of the country. We can't travel on Christmas," Willan said without looking up.

Leiklyn nodded, her skirt wrapping around her legs with the breeze, and she wanted to just stand and enjoy the feel of material against her skin and breathe in the deep freshness of the lake, but she wanted to make this pact with her friends too. The lake wouldn't be the same without them. Blueberry Beach wouldn't be the same without them. Her life wouldn't be the same without them.

That gave her a thought—a brilliant thought.

"My favorite holiday is April Fools' Day. Let's meet then. And we'll flip that holiday on its head, and there won't be a joke. We'll actually be here," Leiklyn said, excited.

"That's perfect!" Tiffany said.

"I have to agree. That's the best day to choose. It's meant so much to us over the years." Willan's tone was serious as always, but there were threads of irony and humor in it as well.

They laughed softly together. There had been plenty of times where they had played jokes on everyone they came in contact with on April Fools' Day.

It was the one holiday they were for sure spending together, and from Christmas on, they were dreaming up things to do that would be fun, that wouldn't get them in trouble, at least not too much, but would still make people laugh and entertain themselves as well.

"Then it's settled. Eighteen years from now, April Fools' Day. We'll meet in the front yard—right here—at the Indigo Inn, and we'll catch up on our lives. And if one of us doesn't make it, the other two will hunt her down like a dog," Leiklyn said, sounding a little threatening but also smiling.

"And drag her back to Blueberry Beach by her hair," Tiffany continued.

"Kicking and screaming all the way, with no mercy," Willan added, with the finality that made their goofiness seem serious.

"Everyone agree?" Leiklyn asked, putting her hand in the middle where they'd formed a natural circle around each other.

"Agree," Tiffany said, putting her hand on top of Leiklyn's.

"Agree," Willan said, adding her hand to the pile.

Together they said, "One, two, three!" then they dropped their hands down and yelled, "Agree!"

Chapter 3

April Fools' Day, eighteen years later

Leiklyn slammed her car door shut and stood, staring at the inn she'd purchased eighteen years ago along with her friends and hadn't laid eyes on since.

She hadn't even told her parents about it.

By the time they'd signed on the house and gotten the key and gone through it just one time, her family had packed up and moved to Chicago.

She supposed her friends hadn't seen it much after that, either, since Tiffany's parents had surprised her with a European tour as a graduation present, and she had gone off on that not long after.

Willan ended up moving out of her house, unable to stand her negative, nasty mother any longer.

And, like Willan had said, that was the last she'd heard of her friends.

She didn't expect them to be here today and hadn't been in contact with them.

That wasn't entirely true.

Willan would probably show up. If she was anything like the girl she had been. She wouldn't make an appointment and not keep it.

Tiffany, on the other hand...she was the golden child, off living the golden child's life, along with some kind of happily ever after, which probably included 2.5 children, the perfect husband, the perfect house, the perfect dog, and the perfect life. Happy, bubbly, and perfect.

Leiklyn reached in her pocket for the key that she had used only once – eighteen years ago.

Mr. Fields had offered to mail his to her when he'd been diagnosed with a brain tumor and gone to live with his son in Chicago. She'd told him not to worry about it, figuring him to be an honest man after caring for the inn with no problems for the last eighteen years.

Although she'd sent him a card and a small gift, she hadn't wanted to have anything to do with Mr. Fields after she'd heard he was going to live with his son. The only son she knew about was Ethan.

Nowadays, Leiklyn wasn't even thinking his name to herself, because the guilt hadn't gone away. New scenery hadn't fixed anything.

Nothing would fix it.

Still, the pain was a little bit more bearable if she kept his name out of her head.

For a year, Indigo Inn had sat empty, with no one taking care of it. Even if they didn't have their pact reunion today, Leiklyn would have had to come back and do something with it. Probably found a real estate agent and sold it.

Although, since she lost her job in HR at an oil company, she supposed she wasn't tied down to Bismarck anymore. She could go wherever she wanted to.

Did she want to come back home to Blueberry Beach?

She hadn't gotten that question fully formed in her mind, let alone answered, when she heard tires on gravel coming out the sandy lane behind her.

She turned, putting her hand over her eyes to shade them, as a sporty SUV pulled to a stop beside her older and much more worn-looking sedan.

A woman with honey brown hair, streaked perfectly with golden blond, big shades, and a classic dress, possibly chosen specifically to hide the extra pounds around her waist and on her hips, stepped out of the vehicle, slamming the door behind her.

"You have to be Tiffany or Leiklyn," the woman said in a slightly cultured voice but one that Leiklyn still recognized. It had that intellectual tint to it.

"Willan?"

"Of course. I'm right on time. You must be Leiklyn, since Tiffany will be late."

"You think Tiffany will come?" Leiklyn said, then she shook her head. "Wait. Willan! Oh my goodness." She threw her arms open and retraced her steps quickly, throwing her arms around her old friend, who only hesitated for a couple of moments before returning the embrace.

They stepped back, their arms sliding down and their hands joining, as they looked each other up and down.

"I guess I should start out by saying you were right. I didn't believe for one second that summer would be the last we saw each other, but you were right."

"I wish I hadn't been. I think that's been one of my greatest faults through the years. I've insisted that I need to be right each and every time I open my mouth, and I finally figured out it drives people away. How could you stand to be friends with me?" Willan said, and while Leiklyn could definitely hear her old friend in her tone, she could also hear a new humbleness that hadn't been there before.

"Most of the time, you *were* right," she said easily.

"I hardly think so. In fact, I know not. I've been wrong so many more times in my life than right."

"Well, I hope you're right about Tiffany," Leiklyn said, not wanting to get sad and melancholy before they even had a chance to catch up on the happy stuff. Obviously, Willan's last eighteen years hadn't been the greatest, and she'd had things happen to her that had scarred her.

Hopefully nothing as bad as what Leiklyn had done. Although, maybe now, with more than two decades between her and her egregiously wicked sin, she could confide to her friends.

Hardly, since they were only going to be here for a little bit. She needed to get back to her kids. And she was sure that Willan had a life as well. Hopefully, she'd get to hear about it before they parted again.

"I'm sure she will be."

"Of the three of us, Tiffany would be the one to—"

She heard the car before she saw it this time, turning her head as a sports car came up over the rise, dust billowing up behind it, the glint of Lake Michigan keeping her from being able to see who was behind the wheel.

Both of them shaded their eyes as the car came to a stop. It was several moments before the driver stepped out.

A sleek haircut and shades with rhinestones on them came into view as a slender body wrapped in a tight shirt and a short skirt appeared and the car door slammed.

"You have to be Leiklyn and Willan, but I can't tell for the life of me which one is which," her voice said, not quite as perky and joyful as it used to be. In fact, if Leiklyn had to say, she'd say it was a fake happy tone and the years had marked Tiffany as well. "Neither one of you have to look so shocked to see me. What? Didn't you think I'd be here?"

Her voice was husky, like a smoker's, and while she smiled, and her words were delivered lightly, there was an undercurrent of hurt, like maybe she knew what her reputation was and had hoped that her friends wouldn't judge her by it.

"I'm surprised that *I'm* even here," Leiklyn said honestly. "I certainly never expected to see either one of you, but the fact that we're all three here..."

"I admit there were years where I totally forgot about this, but it always would pop up in my mind. Usually on April Fools' Day," Willan said.

"I didn't think you ever forgot anything." Leiklyn smiled at her friend.

It felt a little odd to be reunited with people she hadn't seen in eighteen years. It made Leiklyn unsure whether she should just pick up where they left off or try to calculate the years between with the things they had seen and experienced.

No doubt, they were three very different people from the innocents who had sat on the knoll and stared at Lake Michigan and vowed to meet here eighteen years later.

Chapter 4

"Well, we're here. Let's stand on the knoll and face the lake." Tiffany started walking through the sandy yard, which was sparsely covered in high grass, toward the knoll where they had sat on the night of graduation.

Leiklyn glanced at Willan who shrugged and followed.

Leiklyn brought up the rear, noticing that Tiffany stood in one spot and Willan had put plenty of space between them as she stood to the right of Tiffany.

Deciding that there was no point being standoffish, Leiklyn stepped between her two friends and put her arms around them like she had that night so long ago.

"Okay, girls. Were the second eighteen years better than the first?" she asked, hoping she could think of something to say that wasn't outright no.

She supposed her second eighteen years hadn't been terrible, at least she didn't have any more terrible secrets, but she hadn't lived out her faith. She hadn't helped people like she thought she would, and she'd been selfish with her time and her resources. Her main focus throughout her life had been on herself. She couldn't look back and be proud of too much.

Not much beyond her children.

"I can definitely say I'm glad I moved out of my mother's house. And I would never, ever go back." Willan shuddered like her mother had tortured her, which Leiklyn knew to not be true, although she wouldn't want to have lived with Willan's mother either. Being with someone who was constantly depressed and always angry and never satisfied had a tendency to make one constantly depressed, always angry, and never satisfied. "But other than that, the second eighteen years sucked. Excuse my French."

Leiklyn's brows jerked, but she tried to keep her face from showing her shock. Willan was definitely a lot harder, with rougher edges than she had had all those years ago.

"I'd like to talk about it if you want," she said, making her voice gentle.

"We don't have enough time. Plus, I hate complainers. That's all I'd be doing." She nodded her head, looking out at the horizon and the lake that stretched so vast and unfathomable before them. "I'm glad I came. I definitely need to push the reset button in my life. I hate where I'm at, and I'm not going to go in a different direction unless I deliberately change it. Myself."

"It sounds like you just got released from prison. It can't be that bad," Tiffany said, with compassion in her voice but also a touch of sarcasm, as though she found Willan to be a drama queen. "I'm getting divorced from my third husband. Top that," Tiffany added, angling her head forward slightly and spearing Willan with her sharp blue eyes.

When they were in high school, Willan would never have stood up to Tiffany. Not when she looked like that.

But now, her eyes didn't drop, soft and brown, and they actually shed the last of the sarcasm as compassion overtook her gaze. "Sorry. Divorce is never easy. Not for anyone." Her words were whispered soft and low, and they made Leiklyn say, "You've been through it?"

Leiklyn's divorce had been rather unemotional.

She would have stuck it out for her children, but she hadn't really had strong feelings toward her husband. He'd been more interested in his friends and hobbies than he had been in her, and she'd been busy with her job and their kids and hadn't fought for her marriage the way maybe she should have.

When he found someone else, they agreed to split, and that's what they did.

"No. I never married." Willan's chin came out almost as though she didn't want pity for the statement, even though she said it with sadness and regret.

"I should have made you date in high school. You would have learned how to talk to boys, and you definitely would have found someone," Tiffany said, her eyes no longer shooting daggers. But then they dropped. "But that can backfire on you, too."

"Backfire as in a girl ends up with three husbands and none of them a good fit?" Leiklyn asked softly.

"I guess. But also in the sense that a girl ended up doing a lot of things that she wished she wouldn't have."

Leiklyn could commiserate with that. She certainly had things she wished she wouldn't have done, but most of those were in her first eighteen years.

She didn't really regret her marriage, because she had her children. She supposed she could have made a little wiser choice, but she'd settled for the guy who seemed to like her and who didn't seem like he was going to be a wifebeater or bum.

A grand passion...she'd had that, but that was just for teenagers. When a person got older, there was no grand passion; life was about common sense and making good decisions. Passion didn't really have anything to do with it, and definitely not love. Not the kind of love like people in the movies. That was all for teenagers.

Tiffany did not add anything to her statement, so Leiklyn said softly, "I just lost my job. Well, a few months ago, and my unemployment is running out."

The arms of her friends went around her waist, and they both squeezed.

That was what she missed in her life. This feeling of solidarity, that someone was standing beside her, cheering her on, happy for her accomplishments, and ready to catch her if she fell.

She thought when she got married, she would have that same feeling of support and team in her marriage.

Nope.

Her husband was more interested in golfing and hanging out with his buddies than he was in anything that happened to her.

Her bad.

"So I guess it's safe to say that the second eighteen years weren't everything we were thinking they would be," Leiklyn said, her voice void of censure, wondering what they'd done wrong. They'd been so full of hopes and dreams and the optimism of youth, and now she just felt battered and beaten and like it didn't matter what she did, there wasn't anything to be excited about. Just the same old, same old, same old struggle, same old discouragement.

"True for me," Tiffany said in her husky voice that was laced with regrets.

"Me too. I thought high school was terrible. Being an adult is a million times worse." Willan sighed and leaned her body against Leiklyn's. "And these last eighteen were even harder because I didn't have you guys to help me through. I fumbled around a lot on my own, and I'm not nearly as smart as I thought I was."

A few more minutes went by as they stood there, the breeze lifting their hair, the freshness of Lake Michigan filling their lungs, and the sun shining down on them, smiling despite their sad thoughts.

Leiklyn's heart lifted a little. "Things couldn't have been all that bad. I think we're just meeting at a time when we're all three down. There had to have been good times."

"There were. But I think it's the screwups that stick out in our memories. At least mine," Tiffany said. And there was a little bit of bitterness in her tone.

"I agree. You're right. I realized my dream of becoming a librarian, and that was a good thing. The pay is terrible though, and I don't have a family and children, a husband, a man who loves me. That didn't happen." Willan lifted her head off Leiklyn's shoulder and straightened. "But you're right. There was a lot of good in those years too. A lot of learning opportunities in the bad spots."

"That's my mantra, live and learn. What's the point of living if you don't learn? You're just bound to make the same mistakes over and over again, and that's just stupid," Tiffany said, dropping her hand and turning her body to face her friends. "We can change everything. We can. Today. The next eighteen years don't have to be the same. We'll make them better."

"I don't want to think about the next eighteen years. That'll put me in my fifties. That's...old," Leiklyn said, trying not to shudder. Fifty? She didn't even want to think about being that old.

"I think you're right, though. Changes are in order," Willan said. She, too, dropped her hand, only she turned back and faced the inn behind them. "What are you guys planning on doing with this? Obviously, Mr. Fields has been taking care of it, or it would be in much worse disrepair."

"He has," Leiklyn said. "But a year ago, he became ill and went to live with his son in Chicago." She did not mention Ethan's name and prayed her friends would either not remember who Mr. Fields's son was or would not remember that she had an issue with him. Either or both.

Willan tapped her chin with her first finger. "Since he's been gone for a year, someone needs to do something. Either we need to hire someone or...I think I might like to move back to Blueberry Beach. I could move here." Her last words were soft, thoughtful, almost as though she were testing the idea out in her mind at the same time she was speaking it into the air.

"Move back to Blueberry Beach? Isn't that like going backward? Not forward." Tiffany's words held disbelief and maybe a touch of judgment.

But what Willan said had turned in Leiklyn's mind and kind of attached there, feeling right.

"Yeah. Why not? Blueberry Beach is a great place for kids, and I have two," she said, looking at both of her friends and kinda shrugging.

They wouldn't know that. She'd never gotten into social media like the rest of her friends at work. Just something about seeing her ex with his new wife and family made her not want to have anything to do with it. Plus, she was a working mom with two kids. She didn't have time to waste on social media. She'd had a couple of accounts over the years but eventually deleted them, just to keep herself sane.

She stepped forward, turning around and looking at Indigo Inn.

"Mr. Fields kept it in good condition, I know he did. Although I haven't been in. Actually..." She reached her hand in her pocket and pulled out the key. "We can go in right now and look. But...I wouldn't want to do it by myself, but, Willan, if you're seriously thinking about coming back, I'm interested. Maybe we can turn this into something that would make us money. Or maybe we could just live here, but either way, I didn't realize how much I missed living here in Blueberry Beach. Where we grew up and everything is so familiar and beloved."

"So...you two are just going to come back and...what? Live in the manor?"

"I don't know," Leiklyn said, looking at Willan who shrugged her shoulders.

"Normally, I have everything planned out. I don't do things without a seven-step checklist, and three months of planning, but... If I truly want to go in a different direction, I can't keep doing the same things I've been doing, right? Isn't that what you said?"

"Yeah."

"Then I need to throw my planner away. I'm gonna toss out the seven-step checklist. I'm going to do something spontaneous and crazy. I'm going to move back to my hometown and move into Indigo Inn."

"And what will you do to earn a living?" Tiffany asked, as though reminding Willan that life wouldn't be carefree, just because she moved back to the hometown that she grew up in.

"Maybe we can open it up. Or maybe we'll just live there. But I'll figure something out. We own it, and all I would need is money to buy food and pay taxes. I mean, I have to get rid of my apartment, and I don't think my lease is up until the end of the summer."

"I can move as soon as school ends this year," Leiklyn said. "In fact, this is the best time for me to move. I don't have a job, nothing tying me to my home, no commitments, and it would give the kids the summer to get used to things before they start school at Blueberry High. I bet it's exactly the same as it was when we went. Small towns never change."

"I wouldn't be so sure about that. Everything changes," Tiffany said. Although her words came out like she was preoccupied, thinking about something. "You guys are seriously gonna do this?"

"Hey. It's because of you. You're the one who said we can't keep doing the same thing and expect different results."

"That wasn't exactly what I said, and I wasn't talking about going backward. I was talking about moving forward."

"Maybe we didn't move forward when we left here. Maybe we moved backward, and we'll be moving forward by coming back to the starting line again, getting ready to do something different. Something that will..."

"Make us happy?"

"I was gonna say that. But I don't really believe that circumstances make you happy. Even though it's easier to be happy whenever everything is going right. There's no doubt about that."

"Of course. No one is happy when things aren't going right. Happiness definitely depends on your circumstances. So, change your circumstances, and change your happiness." Tiffany crossed her arms over her chest and lifted her chin, as though giving the inn an assessing glance. "I'm gonna get a bunch of money out of my divorce settlement." She sighed, then looked over at Leiklyn. "I haven't paid a cent for this thing over the years. You handled everything."

"It was my idea to begin with. Plus, all I did was pay the taxes, which weren't much, and once in a while, Mr. Fields would call me needing money for some repairs. It was never too much for me to pay, and I just did it."

"Well, the money I'm getting for my divorce settlement can pay for any epic repairs that we need to make before we can open."

"We?" Leiklyn said with a little grin.

"Why not? I might as well. Surely, I can find husband number four around here somewhere," Tiffany said, and she smiled a little. It wasn't like the cares of the world had dropped off her shoulders, but she did look a little younger than she had when she first got out of her car.

"Maybe you should forget about husband number four and do something completely different. Go in a new direction," Willan said with a smile of her own.

"That actually might be a good idea. If I go in a totally opposite direction, I'll have to find a church, volunteer in the nursery, sign up for the cleaning crew, sing in the choir, and join the missionary aid society."

"I don't think they have those anymore," Leiklyn said, lifting her brows at her friend.

"Whatever they have. I should join it all. If I want to completely turn my life around, that's what I need to do."

"You and I need to talk, girl. I don't know what you've been up to, but sounds like you have some interesting stories to tell," Leiklyn said.

"I could probably spin them so they're funny, but I've spent a lot of years getting an education from my experiences when I'd have been better off just listening to a few wise people in my life and my childhood, and I could have avoided a lot of heartache."

"I don't think life is meant to be lived avoiding heartache," Willan said softly. "At least, that's what I figured out. Because that's what I did, and I've ended up alone. I was afraid to take chances, and I avoided the heartache, but I didn't avoid the loneliness and regret."

Leiklyn held her hands up. "Don't look at me to be some kind of middle ground. Because I took the chances, and I have plenty of regrets," she said, then she lifted her chin and jerked it at the inn. "But that's given me wisdom and understanding and compassion, and that's what's gonna make the next eighteen years better than ever."

Tiffany smiled, a true, genuine smile. "So you're moving as soon as school is out, Willan will be here by the end of summer, and I have some loose ends to tie up, but I'll be here sometime, too. Working to fix this grand old inn up, turn it into a bed-and-breakfast, hire the best PR advertising firm in the country, and work to make a killing here in Blueberry Beach."

"No. I'm going to move here, Willan is going to come, and so are you, and we're going to fill this place up with love and laughter, and we're going to have it be known as the most heartwarming hotel in North America. The place where people go when they want to feel loved and cared for."

"You can't forget about the bottom line. That all sounds really nice, but it's pie in the sky unless you're making money to support it. I'm getting some from my divorce, but it's not going to carry us through life on rainbows and unicorns."

"Right. You're right. We're working to make money, and we're also going to be a blessing to people."

"So it's a deal, girls?" Willan asked, thrusting her hand out and angling herself so that they formed a triangle.

"It's a deal. We're going into business together, ladies," Leiklyn said, placing her hand on top of Willan's.

"I can't believe I'm doing this," Tiffany said. "But why not? And I am finding a church too," she said, and while Leiklyn thought it sounded a little sarcastic, she figured it probably wouldn't be a bad idea.

"All right, ladies, here's to the next eighteen years. We're going to make these count."

Their shouts weren't quite as exuberant as they had been on graduation night, but wiser, with more experience behind them, and with the dawning knowledge that life was short.

These were going to be the best eighteen years of her life. Leiklyn was sure of it.

Chapter 5

"Thanks, Miss Iva May."

"You stick around a little bit, honey. I need to write you a check for fixing my roof last week. You left before I could get a hold of you," Iva May said, her cheeks rosy and contrasting with her snow-white hair as she picked his plate up before pouring more coffee in his cup.

"I left because you don't owe me anything." Ethan met her eyes with a grin.

Her lips begin to purse, and she acted like she wanted to put her hand on her hip but couldn't because of the coffeepot.

He widened his grin so that his dimple deepened. "I never paid you for the chicken soup you made me this past winter when I was sick. And you did it three days in a row, although I think it was that home-made bread that really knocked that bug out of me."

"Making chicken soup and homemade bread doesn't begin to compare to fixing someone's roof. You have supplies that need to be paid for."

"You had supplies. Chicken isn't free. Neither is bread. Or whatever it is that you used to make it, which, if you really feel like you owe me and you're just itching to write a check, maybe you could get your hands on the ingredients to make a little more bread instead. That stuff was like manna."

The lady smiled, pleased with his compliments, although she was way too shrewd to be influenced by flattery. Still, his compliments were sincere, and she knew it.

"Well, if you say so, I can make you bread anytime. I can run you some over tonight if you'd like."

"Not this evening. Once I close the hardware store, I need to go out to the Indigo Inn. I have some deliveries to make, and they want some handiwork done around the place." He twisted the handle of his coffee mug. "Maybe they're opening it up. The lady I spoke with didn't say, but it sounds like it."

"Your dad loved the place. How's he doing anyway?" Iva May shifted on her feet but didn't move away from his table at the Blueberry Café.

"He's living with my brother in Chicago. I go down every other week and take him for a couple of days. But he has his house all set up with handicap ramps and that type of thing, and that keeps us from having to put him in a home."

"I thought that's what he'd said when he moved down a year ago. I know he didn't want to leave Blueberry Beach."

"No. He loved the inn." He didn't like talking about his dad, because it was hard to admit that he would soon be gone. "I guess he's slowly fading. Every time I see him, he just looks more frail. It's hard."

He could admit that to Iva May. She wouldn't see that as weakness. Sure enough, the look of compassion and understanding on her face made him feel like she knew exactly what he was going through. It was a good feeling.

"I know when my mom got older, I felt guilty that I couldn't do more. But I also knew she wouldn't want me to feel like that. I'm sure your dad is the same," Iva May said, giving him a last smile before she moved away.

Ethan agreed with Iva May, even if remembering it was hard. His dad wouldn't want him to feel guilty.

He finished up his coffee and then checked the time. He always put a "left for lunch" sign on his shop door when he walked down to the diner in the middle of the day which was usually once a week or once every couple of weeks. It was nice to eat someone's cooking other than his own.

He put a generous tip on the table under his plate, then stood. The summer beach season was upon them, and things were busy, but he supposed life moved around him, and no matter how wild and crazy it got, it just didn't affect him. He was born slow and deliberate, and that's how he did his best work. Especially with his first love—carpentry.

The hardware store paid his bills, and the things he made with wood supplemented that.

Indigo Inn could end up being pretty good income for him over the summer if he played things right with the lady who owned it when he met her tonight.

As he moved to walk out, his eyes caught on a woman sitting at a table beside the window. She sat facing him. Two teenagers sat across from her. A boy and a girl.

Something about the woman looked familiar, but considering he'd grown up in Blueberry Beach and spent every summer here, they could be anyone. She could be a tourist who was here during his childhood perhaps or someone who'd lived here and moved away.

It wasn't uncommon for him to see people he didn't know who looked familiar.

Most uncommon about this woman, though, was the reaction he had to her.

She looked familiar, yes, but his heart kind of jerked and shocked and sped up, and his fingers flexed. The hair on the back of his neck stood up, and he had to consciously remind himself not to turn his steps and start walking toward her.

Odd.

Ethan fought the reaction, shaking his head and disciplining his steps to head to the door, nodding at a family as they came in and walking out under the jingle of the bells.

Funny that the lady was in the back of his head the rest of the day. He supposed he should have stopped and asked her who she was or introduced himself. Found out what was so familiar about her. There was something...

His heart wanted it to be a certain woman, although he knew that was impossible. Not impossible, just highly unlikely since she hadn't been back since she left after high school and probably wouldn't be.

People didn't move back into Blueberry Beach in the middle of their life, thinking it was a good decision.

Some folks retired here, but even that was iffy. The winters were hard, cold, with lots of snow, and the summers were short and hot and busy.

But the small-town atmosphere couldn't be beat, and he couldn't imagine living anywhere else. He definitely didn't want to.

It was seven o'clock when he turned the sign in his store to closed, flipped the lights off, and went out to get in his pickup and drive out to the manor. He'd already loaded the things needed, and he gnawed on some beef jerky on the way.

Lunch had worn off a long time ago, but he wanted to get this done before dark. The lady had mentioned a few odds and ends that needed to be done, and he wanted to be prepared. If she needed estimates and if he needed to look at something, he'd need light.

Thankfully, they were heading into the longest days of the year, and he had several hours of daylight left.

He had been at the inn plenty of times over the last two decades while his dad was caretaker, before he moved back to Blueberry Beach and bought the hardware store. That had been a few years before his dad's decline.

Once again, Ethan wished he had more than his apartment above the hardware store so he could have kept his dad in the town he loved.

He had considered calling up Leiklyn and asking her if he could take his dad's place as caretaker of the inn.

Considering their history, he figured her answer would be no. She'd made it plain that she hated him and blamed him for everything that had happened.

Talk about regrets.

Whoever this woman was he'd talked to, she was obviously the lady that Leiklyn had hired to be the caretaker and replace his father. The lady hadn't seemed to know much about repairing things, and while he didn't laugh about that to himself, it did make him feel a little bit better to think that he could have done a better job if Leiklyn would have hired him in the first place.

Of course, she wouldn't have.

Not with their history.

He pulled in next to a nondescript sedan and looked up to see a girl reading on the porch swing.

It was a beautiful view from their porch—Lake Michigan stretching out in the distance, the lakeshore flowing on either side, and the deep blue of the lake melding into the lighter blue of the sky, the dark ribbon along the horizon where the two met.

He'd never gotten tired of looking at it.

Again, if it hadn't been Leiklyn, he might have asked about purchasing it, although his meager living at the hardware store probably couldn't even begin to touch what this would be worth if it were completely fixed up and ready to accept guests.

He walked up the walk while the girl eyed him suspiciously. He got the feeling she'd like to run but knew it would be considered rude.

Before he made it to the top of the stairs and stepped on the porch, a woman came to the door.

She pushed it open, and he realized immediately it was the woman from the diner. Funny how the Lord worked things sometimes.

He didn't have too much time to think about it though, focusing instead on keeping his heart rate under control, making sure he didn't drool, shutting his mouth, and trying not to stare.

Her eyes were green, her hair a golden blond, and her figure not willow thin like a teenager's but shaped more like an hourglass.

She smiled, a generic, professional smile, and held out her hand. "I'm Leiklyn Weaver, and you must be the owner of the hardware store whom I spoke with on the phone earlier."

Ethan really had thought that he wouldn't stare. He had thought he could keep his mouth closed and act professionally.

That was before she said her name.

Leiklyn was not a common name.

He had to be looking at the only woman he'd ever loved.

Some men seem to go from woman to woman without too much trouble, almost like one was just as good as another.

Or maybe they just hadn't found the one that hit them in the solar plexus, stole their last breath and their brain, and made them do stupid things, all the while wishing they could do it longer and more, loving that breathless feeling, willing to do anything to stay beside her, spend his life working to make her happy. Knowing that his happiness would come just by being around her, in her presence, just with a smile once in a while.

His mouth was dry, and he couldn't find anything to swallow to try to take the scratch out of his throat, so he sounded a little hoarse when he reached out and took a hold of her hand, knowing how it would feel when he did.

"I'm Ethan. I guess you probably don't remember me, but I remember you."

Just like he thought, grabbing a hold of her hand was like grabbing a hold of a Fourth of July firecracker, one that was lit and throwing sparks everywhere. Still, she was the one who pulled away, because he would never pull away.

If it had been up to him, he would never have let go.

At least he had the pleasure of knowing he surprised her. It was probably the beard. He kept it trimmed short, but he didn't look anything like the boy he had been in school. Broader shoulders, definitely more muscles, and not as skinny. Maybe there was some wisdom in his eyes, definitely more patience, but he hardly thought he had more self-control when it came to Leiklyn.

Not when he wanted to rub his hand up and down his pant leg and shove it in his pocket to try to forget about the burning sensation that he still felt even though she'd let go seconds ago.

"Ethan Fields." Leiklyn said his name like she was reading the time of the doomsday clock and there were only seconds left.

There were a couple of moments of unguardedness on her face which he was thankful for because it then shut down into a polite mask as though she were looking at a stranger.

"Thank you for delivering the items I asked for. Tell me what I owe you, and I'll write you a check, but I think we both know we can't work together."

It had been twenty years that the secret lay heavy between them.

He'd never told anyone. He doubted she had. Not from the way she was looking at him. He hated it was that way. He hated that at the time, too. He'd wanted to do something, something else, but they'd both been young and scared and they'd done the only thing they knew to do.

He certainly lived with regret. He couldn't imagine how she must feel.

"If you want anything done, you'll have to hire someone from Chicago to come up. You know how summers are in Blueberry Beach. I actually didn't really have time, but my dad loved this inn. So did I. And I was making the time. I still will. But if you don't want me to, I understand."

Chapter 6

Leiklyn stared at the man in front of her. He bore no resemblance, or very, very little, to the boy she'd known. Her chest felt like a furnace turned up on high, and her heart was pounding hard and fast.

She managed to not wipe her sweaty palms down her pant legs, but she wanted to.

She couldn't swallow because her mouth felt like it was stuffed with cotton, and it took a great bit of effort to get her whirling thoughts in order.

For so long, she'd programmed herself to avoid him. If not to hate him, at least to know that there could never be anything between them, even if he had seemed like he was exactly perfect for her.

Maybe that's why she'd settled in her marriage. Because no one would ever live up to Ethan. Foolish, since she could see where that got her.

Even though all of her instincts were telling her to run, to turn around and slam the door, to tell him no thank you, she'd rather live in a rundown house for the rest of her life than spend two seconds in his presence, she knew that was childish.

Surely, she'd done some maturing over the last two decades, and she could face this person who knew her deepest, darkest secret without acting like a total moron.

Which is how she felt she would be acting if she did what she wanted to.

It wasn't his fault. It wasn't right for her to punish him as though it were.

Drawing herself in and up, trying to whip her emotions into some semblance of maturity, she tried to not look like she was scared to death and to look like she was a mature woman in her mid-thirties and not a callow teen.

"I'm sorry, Ethan. I spoke rashly."

She could do this. She could pretend that there was nothing be-tween them, instead of everything.

"I'm sorry about your father. He did a great job of taking care of this place for years."

"I know. I helped him. That's probably another reason why I'm a good man for the job."

His words were dispassionate but not unkind. Maybe he didn't even remember.

He had to remember.

"I had heard he was living with his son in Chicago. I thought that was you. I didn't realize he had another son."

"A lot of people don't. My dad was married before, for a short time, and my brother is a lot older than me."

Mr. Fields must have had two relationships not work out, since Ethan hadn't had a mother in his house growing up.

Hardly a subject she could comment on now.

"I see," she said, not wanting to say anything that might hint at the subject she most certainly did not want to talk about.

Would it be better to get it out in the open?

Her mind nudged her, and she shushed the little voice that wanted to take her far, far out of her comfort zone and put her somewhere in a land she wouldn't recognize.

Her children didn't know. What kind of example would that have been to them?

"Listen, I can see you're uncomfortable. And I know why," Ethan began, but she put a hand up, glancing over where her daughter had been sitting on the porch swing.

Her spot was empty, and her daughter was nowhere in sight.

Myla hadn't been very happy with the move, but more than that, there seemed to be something else going on with her that Leiklyn hadn't been able to figure out. Normally, she and Myla had a great relationship and talked all the time. But lately, Myla hadn't wanted to have too much to do with her.

At first, Leiklyn had been chalking it up to a typical teenager getting older, but it seemed like there was something more pressing or serious on Myla's mind.

She hadn't had a chance to figure it out, with the move and with needing to get the place fixed up so they could open it and make money before her unemployment completely ran out, since, while Tiffany's money would fix the place up, she could hardly pay herself out of it. She needed to take the time to really try to sit down with Myla and make sure that it was just moving to a new place that was bothering her and not something more serious.

"Let's not go there," she said, when Ethan stopped talking at her upraised hand.

"It might be a good idea to clear the air between us."

"I can't deny that, but right now isn't the time. My children have no idea, and I don't want them to know."

"You have children?" He seemed interested, but not excessively curious.

"Two. A girl who is fifteen and my son is fourteen."

"So you and your husband came back to run this?"

A lie sat on the tip of her tongue, just vibrating there. All she had to do was open her mouth and let it out, and that would take care of every problem between Ethan and her.

But it was a small town, and a lie would be found out almost immediately, then he'd know exactly why she told it or at least suspect.

"I'm divorced," she said, her words sounding final and not inviting any more comments.

Ethan had been a wonderful person. Even at fifteen, he was kind and considerate and mature beyond his years. She couldn't fault him, not in any way. If anything, the fault was hers.

Plus, beyond the terrible, awful memory, there were beautiful ones. Forbidden, yes, but still beautiful.

Maybe that's why she had to hold herself so tightly closed. Because Ethan was the only man she'd ever met who felt so perfectly right to her in every way.

He'd changed. She'd changed. It wouldn't be the same any longer, and she had to keep her heart locked up tightly until it accepted that.

"I see," he said. If there was relief in his tone or on his face, he hid it well. "So... Are you going to hire down to Chicago for this, or do you want me to unload the stuff I brought and look at what needs to be done?"

"Please unload your things. I'm sorry I didn't make you feel welcome immediately. The memories I have concerning you are memories I'd prefer to stay hidden. I never told anyone about what happened." She lowered her voice in case her kids were listening so they wouldn't hear.

They were the only ones at the inn currently, other than Ethan, of course, and while she knew her children didn't think she was perfect, they did think she was a moral person who did right. She didn't want them to know how wicked she really was.

"Neither did I." His gaze shifted a little, his eyes narrowing. "That's not something a man goes around telling people."

"We were both kids. You were hardly a man."

"I guess you're right. A man would have handled things differently."

He didn't say he was a man now and regretted what they'd done, but he didn't really need to. His look said it all.

"I agree. I'm a child no longer as well." Her words were soft but firm. He might as well know she felt the exact same way, and if she had to do it over again, she would most definitely be doing it differently.

"Dad always kept all of his stuff in a shed out back. Is it okay if I unload these things there, then I'll be around for you to show me what needs to be done?"

"That's fine. I'll go tell the kids what I'll be doing and finish clearing supper off the table. Come on around the back. You can use the back door that leads to the kitchen when you're ready. It's unlocked."

"As I recall, the lock doesn't work."

She smiled a little. "You recall correctly."

"If you're going to be living here, I'll put that on my list of things to fix."

"That's not necessary. Blueberry Beach has always been a safe town. I'm more concerned about getting things ready for the guests and passing inspection."

"Your safety isn't important?"

"I said I wasn't worried about it," she said, meeting his gaze, his brown eyes showing concern.

"Then for the sake of your children, fix the lock on the kitchen door."

He had her there. It wasn't that she didn't care about her children's safety; it's just that Blueberry Beach was safe. "They have locks on their bedroom doors. All of those work."

"As will the back door. I won't charge you for that, just in case it's the money you're worried about. It's just something that should be done in order for you to be safe."

His eyes, while still kind and concerned, were firm, and his gaze didn't waver.

She wasn't going to fight about it. She'd been uncomfortable the door wouldn't lock anyway, but she hadn't got around to trying to figure out how to fix it. He was doing her a favor, and she was being a brat again.

"Thank you. Of course I'll pay you for it. It needs to be done, and I appreciate you making sure we're safe."

He didn't say anything, although his jaw flexed and he inclined his head ever so slightly. "Since I insisted, I won't charge you. Not for the lock. Not for the labor. And that's final."

"That's very kind of you, but we do actually have a budget for fixing things up. And it's not going to be just me. Tiffany and Willan are pitching in as well, although they couldn't move here as quickly as I could."

"I should have known you three would be together again. Blueberry Beach doesn't know what it's in for," Ethan said. The serious look had dissipated, and he was almost smiling.

"We're all older, wiser, and hopefully a little more mature than we used to be. I think in general, we'll be assets to Blueberry Beach and not the whirlwinds we might have been in our youth."

"I'm sure. I suppose we'll never completely shed our childhood though."

"I guess you didn't. Your father owned the hardware store, and now you do. I hadn't realized that either." She'd finally put it all together. A few years after she'd left Mr. Fields had bought the hardware store that he'd managed when they were kids. He'd renovated the apartments upstairs, but never moved out of Indigo Manor. It made sense that Ethan had bought his dad out.

"Yeah, that happened a while ago. Dad was ready to retire, and I was ready to settle down."

She'd forgotten that he'd gone away after school. Not to college or trade school, like most of their class had. But to actually do something in the world.

It didn't surprise her then, and it surprised her even less now. He was just the kind of man who was always looking for things he could do to help other people. He'd had that maturity even as a youth.

"All right." He took his hand out of his pocket and turned. "I'll be unloading stuff if you need me."

Her mouth spoke before she gave it a thought. "We have some leftovers from supper. Do you want me to put some together for you?"

What was she thinking? She wanted to be nice, but she didn't want to be buddy-buddy with him. Not really.

Although, Ethan would make an excellent friend. Loyal and stead-fast and always with a mind to help. His friends would be blessed. Except she didn't think she could really be his friend without wanting more.

Even now, with everything that had happened between them, she felt the buzz of attraction, and that was probably why those words came out of her mouth without her permission. She wanted to be closer, spend time with him, get to know the man he had become as she remembered the boy he had been.

"I don't want to put you out. But I haven't eaten."

"We'll plan on it whenever you come in."

"Thanks," he said, stepping off the porch and walking to his truck.

As much as she wanted to stand and watch him walk away, she didn't.

She turned before he'd reached it and walked in the house, pulling her phone out of her pocket and texting her kids. It had become their default method of communication since the house was so large they didn't hear her when she called for them. Although both of them knew that if they were going to leave the building and the yard around it, she wanted to know.

Her children hadn't grown up by the lake, and while the waters often looked placid and calm, that could change in a heartbeat, and even if it didn't change, people who grew up around the lake drowned in it every year. You had to respect the water. Part of that was letting people know where you were and not going out in it without someone with you.

I'll be showing our new handyman around and letting him know the jobs I have on my list.

She sent the text while walking down the double hallway that ran through the length of the house and turning into the kitchen. There were two front parlors, a library, several smaller rooms which could be reading nooks or sitting rooms, a ballroom on the opposite side from the kitchen that took up most of the south wing downstairs, and a large dining room connected to the kitchen.

It was a gorgeous house and one she loved.

Hopefully, their guests would fall in love with it too and spread the word and come back year after year to stay.

The microwave was beeping with the plate of food she'd put in it for Ethan when he rapped on the back door and pushed it open without waiting for her to answer.

"I figure if it's not locked, you're not expecting people to stand and wait until you're free to open it," he said as he walked in.

"I suppose that makes sense," she said, going to the microwave and lifting his plate out. They'd had meatloaf and mashed potatoes, and she'd thrown a large helping of peas on the side.

Back when they'd been together, she didn't remember him not liking anything, but they'd mostly eaten burgers and fries. Typical teenage fare. They hadn't spent much time at either one of their houses.

He wiped his feet on the mat in front of the door while she set his plate on the large, heavy wood kitchen table.

"Come on in and sit down. I'm sorry you felt like you had to rush in here without eating first."

"I wanted everything done for the day, so once I get back home, I'm finished." He grinned a little. "I like it out here. Maybe I was eager to come out and see the changes a year made."

"I guess you probably spent a good bit of time here with your dad." It was something she hadn't even considered.

"We did. I just have the apartment over the hardware store, so when we got together, for holidays and also Sunday dinners, we usually ate here."

"It's funny, but I bought this just about the time I graduated and just before I left town for good. You've probably spent more time here than I have." She huffed out a laugh. "In fact, I know you have. I barely walked through it before we moved in last week."

"It's a grand old place. Fixed up right, it could be gorgeous."

"I don't think we have the budget to fix it up to its former glory, but I think we can make it look pretty good."

"What time frame are you looking at?" he asked as he picked up his fork.

She noted that he bowed his head for just a moment, and she shook that thought away. That's the kind of boy he'd been. The kind of girl she had been.

She supposed she hadn't gotten too far away from that, and it looked like he hadn't either. The thought made something else warm her chest. The buzzing attraction was still there of course, but this additional feeling enhanced that.

She knew spending time with him would not be a good idea. There were plenty more things that she would notice and admire. Not good.

"We're hoping to have it up to inspection and able to have guests this summer."

His head popped up, and she smiled. "I know. That's a pretty ambitious time frame. But your dad kept it in really great condition, and I'm planning on hiring out." She lifted her brows and gave a conceding look. "From Chicago, if necessary, to get everything finished."

"I see."

"When Willan and Tiffany and I talked about it, we decided that we wouldn't be able to get all of the rooms finished. There are some plumbing issues, and all of them need to be painted, and some of them need to be completely redone. That's kind of what I'm hoping you'll do."

"Yeah. It's been years since I walked through it. Dad kept the kitchen in good shape, and the dining room isn't bad. But he didn't try to keep up with all the bedrooms. There were too many, and it was going to take too much money."

"Exactly. So, the plan is to be working on it as we have guests. Which might be a little bit difficult, but I'm working to try to make it happen. I don't want to miss the summer tourist season."

He swallowed, his food almost gone. "This would be gorgeous at Christmastime too. Michigan has a beautiful fall, even if we don't have the trees as a draw like New England."

"Well, people boat into the fall, but there is also the hospital, and that's year-round. Not that people are looking for a great vacation there, but we had some interest already."

"I bet. I hadn't thought of that." He scraped the last of the food off his plate before he stood. "Thank you. I eat at the diner once in a while, but it's usually a sandwich. When Dad was here, it was usually me cooking. I never make anything this fancy. It was delicious, and I appreciate it."

"Meatloaf and mashed potatoes is not fancy," she said, meeting him halfway between the table and the sink and taking his plate from him.

She kept her eyes cast down, still not sure how she was going to handle this. Every second she spent with him, she remembered why she'd liked him in the first place, and she liked him even more now.

Part of her was already asking why they couldn't be more. Why not? What was stopping them?

So they'd done something terrible together. He hadn't told anyone, and neither had she, and it was a secret that might bind them together. It didn't have to tear them apart.

When she used logic like that, she wondered why she'd quit talking to him in the first place. And why she thought it was such a big deal. They could have gone through it together and become stronger.

Except it was a terrible thing for them to have done.

"I'd offer you dessert, but I don't have any. I'm sorry."

"Not a problem. That was good enough. It doesn't need to be topped off with anything."

"Well, that's kind of you to say, but maybe next time." What was she saying? There wouldn't be a next time. She had to remember that.

She set his plate in the sink. "Follow me, and I'll show you where I'd like to start."

Chapter 7

The next day, Ethan was standing at the paint area in his shop, checking inventory and taking down a few notes, when the bell rang, and he looked up to see what looked like a young teenager walk into the shop.

The kid was pale and didn't look like he got out much, and there was something about his nose, maybe, and his emerald eyes that made Ethan think that this might be Leiklyn's son.

At least, it was a little early in the season for tourists, and he knew there was a new kid in town.

That was just him putting two and two together and maybe getting five. Regardless, he looked at the kid and nodded his head. "Good morning."

The kid swallowed and said, "Good morning," in the crackly voice that youthful boys often had, especially when they were nervous.

"Can I help you with something?" Ethan asked. "It's a beautiful morning to get started on a project," he added conversationally as he set the book he was writing in on top of the lower shelf of paint, where he'd stopped, and turned and walked toward the kid.

"I'm looking for a job," he said.

Ethan nodded his head, thinking that he'd already hired the same kid who'd worked for him last summer. And he didn't really need anyone else. Although, maybe...

"I'm Ethan," he said, holding out his hand. "I don't recognize you from around town. Are you new?"

"My mom just moved into the Indigo Inn with my sister and me. She told me I needed to find a job for myself or she was going to make me work for her, so I looked at the shops along Main Street and figured I'd start here."

"Because you have experience in working at a hardware store?" he asked, only half paying attention to the kid's answer. His first impression had been right; this was Leiklyn's son.

The idea shook him. Imagining what could have been. Might have been. He was a good-looking boy, and while he looked a little out of his element, it took a certain kind of bravery to walk in and ask for a job the way he had. Ethan could admire and respect that.

Leiklyn's son.

"No, sir."

"You do projects on your own?"

"No, sir."

Ethan nodded. He'd kinda figured when he'd shaken the boy's hand. It had been soft. "So what are you interested in?"

"Back where I came from, I was pretty good with electronics. I dabbled some in computer programming and that type of thing."

"So...a hardware store is kind of an odd place for you to be," Ethan pointed out.

"Someone said the only video game store in town closed, and there aren't any computer stores in Blueberry Beach, so this was the next best thing."

"I see," Ethan said. He supposed it might have been. There was a surf shop, and a diner, and the Little People Shop. A craft store and the secondhand store, and a few others scattered up and down Main Street. He supposed the hardware store really was the closest thing to electronics, even if it was a stretch.

"Are you still in school?" he asked.

"Yeah."

"You want a summer job. A temp position," Ethan said.

"Yeah. I guess," the kid said.

"I guess you didn't tell me your name."

"It's Trent."

"Well, Trent. Your mom just offered me a job last night, fixing up the inn. It's going to be a big one, and I was thinking I was going to need help. She wants it done kinda fast, and it's probably a little bigger than what I can handle on my own. Are you interested in helping?" He hoped he wasn't wrong when he'd judged the kid to be a good worker and a fast learner. If he was good with electronics, he was probably good with his hands, and if he had a good attitude, he could learn anything Ethan could teach him.

"Who's gonna run the store while you're working at the inn?"

"Same kid who worked here last year. He's already been to see me, and I told him the job was his. Fixing up the manor is all I've got."

Trent shuffled his feet and looked down. "You know you'll need to teach me whatever I have to do."

Ethan flexed his jaw. He'd be working with Leiklyn's son. Irony, right? "I guess I haven't taught too many people, but I think I can do it. I don't typically get angry and throw things, anyway."

"I don't know. I don't even have the first idea of how to do what Mom wants. She tried to talk me into helping her, and I wasn't even sure I could run a paintbrush good enough to make everything look okay for paying customers."

"We'll start you off somewhere where it doesn't matter. A closet or something, and we'll work you out from there."

It's what his dad had done with him. He'd started off drywalling closets. Which, barring something with actual curves in it, were one of the harder things to drywall anyway. If a person could do a closet, they could do anything. It's what his dad had said.

"How about we try for a week or two? I won't get upset if you decide the work isn't for you, because I will expect you to work. And hard. It will be long hours, and you won't have much free time to goof off during the summer. Not if we're going to get this job done for your mom."

The kid nodded. "I guess I kind of like it. Mom's worked hard to take care of us, and she's never said anything, but I kinda feel like she feels like it would be nice if I stepped up and became the man of the family."

"Has your dad been gone long?" That was a personal question, one he probably shouldn't be asking. But he wanted to know. Wanted to know everything there was to know about Leiklyn.

Seeing her last night, having her offer him food when she definitely didn't have to, then warming it up and serving it with a smile, had made him realize that she'd never really left his heart. He just closed it up tight and tucked it away.

"He left when Myla was a baby. I guess I was too. I don't really remember him much."

"He was involved with you?"

"Some. He sent money. We haven't seen him much since he got active and involved with his new family and wasn't very interested in us."

Leiklyn had been a single mom for a long time. He hadn't known.

Would it have changed anything if he had?

He wasn't sure. Couldn't say. Thought maybe it would have, but it was too late to tell now.

"I was getting things in order today. Buddy, the kid that I hired, is starting tomorrow, and I'll probably spend the day with him, reminding him of everything he did last year, making sure he's going to be okay. The day after that, I was planning on starting at your mom's inn. That work for you?"

"Yeah. It does."

"I figured I'd work from six until six. That going to be too much for you?" He was actually planning on working longer than that, but if the kid wasn't used to working, he probably wouldn't be able to keep up.

"I think so. I guess I'll need to pick a really loud ring for my alarm on my phone."

"Did you get yourself up for school?"

"I did, but it didn't start until 8:30. Six o'clock is a lot different. I'll have to get up at...5:30 or so."

Ethan grinned. "You'll get used to it. How about I pack a lunch for both of us the first day, so that'll take a little of the pressure off you and you can sleep in just that much longer."

Trent smiled, not a huge smile but the kind of smile that said maybe he was going to get along with him after all.

"Thanks," he said. "I don't like onions," he added, almost as an afterthought.

"That's fine. I'll put double on my sandwich and keep them off yours."

"That's a deal."

"Don't you want to know what I'm going to pay you?" Ethan asked, his lips curving up at Trent's surprised look.

"I guess it doesn't matter. I got a job. And it wasn't as hard as I thought it was going to be. Maybe you'll want to wait to pay me until you know for sure that I can do the work."

"The work I do isn't hard. You just have to be diligent."

Diligent wasn't a word that got tossed around a whole lot, but Trent seemed to know what it meant, because he nodded, shoulders square.

"I'll try my hardest," he said.

"Good. I guess your mom's business is depending on it."

That made his eyebrows go up. It probably gave him plenty to think about, too.

They said goodbye, and the bell jingled after him as the kid walked out.

Leiklyn's son. He never in a million years thought he'd spend a summer working with Leiklyn's son, but he'd always heard that God moved in mysterious ways. It was certainly easy to believe after the encounter he'd just had.

Shaking his head, Ethan walked back over to the paint shelf and picked his notebook up. Something told him this summer was going to be different than any other summer in his life before.

Chapter 8

"I'm so glad you agreed to come to my house for tea," Iva May said as she smiled at Leiklyn and Myla who were sitting at her kitchen table.

Leiklyn smiled, feeling warm and loved. Iva May just had that way about her, always had, that made her feel like she was welcome and wanted.

Not to mention that today was Ethan's first day at the inn, and she had jumped at the excuse to not be there when she stopped at the diner yesterday and Iva May had invited her and Myla for tea at her house on her day off.

"It was kind of you to invite us. I haven't had tea in a really long time. That's just not something that a mom with two kids and a full-time job gets to do very often."

That was the truth. She worked, ran her kids to practices, and tried her hardest to keep up with laundry and dishes and meals and everything else. It hadn't been easy.

At least she hadn't struggled for money. Her ex might not care to see his kids, but he'd always sent his child support payments.

"You know your mom worked in the diner when she was a kid," Iva May said, looking at Myla who had been unusually silent. Or usually silent, as in the past two months, she'd pretty much quit talking. At least quit talking to Leiklyn.

Iva May had always been like a grandmother to Leiklyn, even though they'd lost touch over the years. Maybe Myla would be comfortable with her and able to open up about whatever was bothering her, especially if it was anything serious.

Leiklyn recalled going through times as a teenager where she just withdrew into herself, thinking about things and trying to make sense of the world.

There were also times where she felt like her mother had no clue what was going on in her life and was the last person she wanted to talk to. Somehow, she just thought that was what Myla's problem was. She also figured it had been made worse by the move.

No teenager wanted to leave their friends and everything that was familiar and have to start over at a new school and a new place somewhere else.

"Being a waitress is hard. Your mom was really good at it."

"I think it'd be fun. Writing down people's orders in a book and bringing food out to them. I guess I don't see what's hard about that."

Leiklyn shared a knowing look with Iva May over Myla's head.

"One of the things that makes being a waitress hard is that people get upset over things you have no control over. If things are busy and you can't get to them right away, or if the cook burns the food, or makes it wrong, or puts mustard on it when they asked for ketchup." Iva May shrugged. "Most of the time, the people who come to the diner are really kind, but everyone has bad days. When you're looking forward to a good meal, and it's been ruined because you didn't want it toasted and it is, I guess sometimes that's just the last straw that breaks the camel's back. And people unload on the waitress."

As Iva May spoke, she lifted the teakettle from the stove and poured three full cups of tea.

She set them carefully on the table and gave everyone a spoon.

"I guess I hadn't thought of that."

"Even for adults, it's hard to see outside of our knowledge circle and realize that things that are important to us don't mean much of anything to some other people and that we have no clue about things that are extremely important to others."

Leiklyn was a little hesitant to join the conversation since Myla seemed to be talking to Iva May comfortably. But she added, "Iva May used to say all the time, we know what we know, but we don't know what we don't know, and that's the problem." She laughed a little. "I didn't always understand that when I was younger, but it's come back to me more than once as I've gone through my life, and I've realized how very true it is."

"What does that mean?" Myla said with her nose scrunched up.

"It means," Iva May said, "that, obviously, whatever you know, you know that you know it, and it's not a surprise to you. But just like now where you had no idea what might make a waitress's life hard, you didn't know that, and you didn't know that you didn't know it. Does that make a little sense?" she asked, stirring her tea and smiling sweetly at Myla.

Myla nodded slowly. She'd always been a thinker, and smart too, taking after her father.

Even after all the years that had passed, there was a little pang in Leiklyn's chest when she thought about her ex. She'd wanted to have the two-parent home with the kids and the all-American family. Him cheating had stolen all of that from her.

At the time, she'd placed a lot of the blame on herself. If she'd been happier. If she'd been skinnier. If she'd been more beautiful. If she'd been a better conversationalist or had given him whatever it was that he didn't have that he found with the woman he'd left her for.

But after he left that woman, pregnant, and moved on to someone else, she slowly came to the conclusion that it was not her fault.

Still, she supposed the scars would always be tender.

"I wasn't trying to talk you out of being a waitress though," Iva May said as she put half a teaspoon of sugar in her tea and passed the sugar container to Leiklyn, who passed it on to Myla. She had a terrible sweet tooth, but tea was one thing that she enjoyed with absolutely nothing added to it.

Hiding a smile, she watched as Myla put three teaspoons of sugar in her tea.

"The diner can always use help in the summer, and you might meet some friends that way. The girls from the ice-cream shop sometimes run over to grab a coffee or a sandwich at lunch. They're really nice, and I think you'd enjoy spending time with them."

Myla nodded, but she didn't say much, staring at her tea and stirring.

Leiklyn gave Iva May an apologetic look. That's how Myla had been treating her lately. Not rude necessarily, because she responded to everything Leiklyn said, but she just didn't have too much to say.

"So I heard Ethan is going to be helping you out at the inn?" Iva May said, giving Leiklyn an understanding look.

"He is."

"Back when you were a teenager, working at the diner, I remember you didn't care for him too much. It's funny how our perspective shifts as we get older. Ethan is a good man."

Leiklyn didn't miss Myla's head jerking up at the mention that there was a boy her mother didn't like when she was a teenager.

Hopefully, she didn't start asking Ethan why, although she hardly doubted that Ethan would say anything to her daughter without checking with her first. He didn't seem like the kind of man who wanted to one-up people. Or who would want to cause problems between her and her child.

"That's what I've heard. He was a good kid then too. I guess I was the one with the problem."

That seemed to be the story of her life. It was her fault she was divorced, her fault that things turned out the way they did with Ethan.

Actually, it probably was. Maybe if she hadn't been such an idiot, they would have been able to stay together. Ethan wouldn't have left her for someone else. He was the kind of man who stuck.

"Don't be so hard on yourself. Everyone makes mistakes," Iva May said, patting Leiklyn's hand. Leiklyn almost missed it, but out of the corner of her eye, Myla's eyes widened and then narrowed.

She didn't miss the sound of her spoon clattering to the table though.

"If it's okay with you, I'd like to be excused and go walk down by the beach, please," Myla said, softly but urgently, like there was something she just remembered she had to do and she needed to get it done immediately.

Even though Leiklyn's brows pushed together, she nodded. "If that's okay with you, Iva May?"

"Of course. I'd love to chat with you some more, Myla. Sometime when you have time, I'd like to get to know you."

Myla nodded, pushing back from the table.

"And if you'd like a job at the diner, I'm sure you can have one. As long as it's okay with your mom."

"I think Mom wants me to help her at the manor. Now that Trent's working with Mr. Ethan, Mom thinks it's a good idea for us all to pitch in."

She took her teacup to the sink and set it down before murmuring a "thank you" and walking out with her head down, her strides long.

"She looks so much like you," Iva May said as the door slammed shut behind Myla.

"She has her father's intelligence, thankfully. But I'm not sure what's gotten into her lately. For the last several months, she's just been...quiet. It used to be that she and I talked about everything. I could hardly get rid of her. Not that I wanted to, but it seemed like every time I turned around, I tripped over her and she wanted to talk to me about something. Even if it was the color of nail polish she should paint her fingernails that day."

"And then they grow up, and they quit talking."

"That's exactly what I was thinking. But when you said that about making mistakes..." Leiklyn set her spoon down carefully and looked at her tea for a moment, gathering her thoughts. "Myla's reaction just gave me...the idea that there was something else. But I have no idea what it could be, and the couple of times I've tried to ask, she's either shut down or found an excuse to walk away."

"I guess all you can do is keep trying. You can't make her talk to you."

"I know. You're right." Leiklyn sighed. "It's just...with everything that's been going on, the move, starting with the manor, and...working with Ethan."

"There was something between you two if I recall correctly," Iva May said carefully. She waited for Leiklyn to nod before she added, "It must have ended badly, since you didn't even want to hear his name in your presence."

"That's true, there *was* something between us." She still felt it. Still felt the attraction, but more than that, it felt like he was the man who complemented her like no one else. Someone who could understand her, and someone who she wanted to know better. There was just so much that pulled her to him, like there always had been. "And it's true it ended badly and I probably handled it about as poorly as anyone could ever be expected to handle anything."

"But that's over and done now, and you put it behind you, since he's working at the manor with you, right?"

"I guess. We never really talked about it, although he wanted to. I suppose we should. Just to clear the air and get things settled."

"You know, through my life, I've often thought to myself I should do this or that or the other thing, and time gets away from me, and years end up going by. Decades even. And then I end up with the big secret that the whole world should know, that I'm embarrassed and ashamed about, and that I still put off telling anyone about." Iva May rubbed her fingers over Leiklyn's hand one more time then pulled her hand away and picked up her teacup. She looked over the rim at Leiklyn. "Don't be me."

Leiklyn was too surprised to say anything. Iva May had a secret? One she was ashamed of? She was telling Leiklyn not to be her?

She couldn't even imagine since Iva May just didn't seem like the kind of person to have anything secret or wrong in her past. She was so sweet and always full of wisdom and kindness.

"I've shocked you, honey. I didn't mean to. Let's talk about other things. How's your family?"

They chatted for an hour or so before Leiklyn excused herself, thanking Iva May for the tea and for the friendship. It was a blessing to see people you'd not talked to for decades and meet them again and just pick back up right where you were. Iva May was one of those people, although, to be fair, Blueberry Beach was that kind of town. The kind of town that felt like an easy landing for a hard fall. Exactly what she needed right now.

Chapter 9

Ethan had to hand it to Leiklyn. In the week that he'd been coming to the Indigo Inn and working, she had been there the entire time, working just as long hours as he did and sometimes longer since she was working when he got there and was still working when he left.

Other than taking off for a couple of hours one afternoon to meet with Iva May, according to Trent, who was a great source of information if Ethan were trying to get information about Leiklyn. Which, typically, he tried not to do. There was something that wasn't quite right about pumping a woman's child for information about her.

Even if Trent was almost old enough to be considered an adult.

"I screwed all the drywall in, Mr. Ethan. I just have that one small piece to do, and you said you'd show me how?" Trent pulled Ethan out of his thoughts as they worked in the second upstairs bedroom.

The first hadn't needed much done to it other than a little bit of scraping and some paint.

Leiklyn had said that to begin with they would paint everything a creamy white and use accents to bring the colors out.

That made picking paints easy. Whether it was convenience or on purpose, she bought all of her supplies at his hardware store.

He'd given her a pretty good discount, as much as he could afford, and the first bedroom was finished. The second needed a lot more, and while, after a week of painting and applying finish to the floor, Trent was pretty good at both of those jobs, he was new to drywall.

"Do you have the razor knife I gave you?" Ethan asked. The razor knife had been his gift to Trent the first day they were together, along with the lunch he'd made—no onions.

They hadn't had too much reason to use it, but for drywall, it would definitely come in handy.

"It's right here," Trent said, pulling the razor knife out of his pocket.

"Let me show you how we're going to measure that piece, and then we'll use our razor knives to cut it."

Ten minutes later, he'd taught Trent the same thing his father had taught him at a much younger age, although watching someone do it and doing it yourself were two different things.

Thankfully, there was a small linen closet in the bathroom of the room they were working on, and Trent would have lots of practice cutting pieces of drywall into smaller shapes to fit that area.

After that, there was the spackling to learn how to do, which was a different skill in and of itself.

Leiklyn's kid was a good learner, and while he had absolutely no experience and no skills at what they were doing, he had a good attitude, and that meant more than anything.

"Are you guys too busy to take a break in here?" Leiklyn appeared at the door with a tray of fruit in her hands.

"If it includes food, we're not too busy for anything," Ethan said, throwing a grin at Trent, which Trent returned. The kid was a typical teenage boy, which meant he pretty much inhaled anything edible within one hundred yards of his skinny body.

Carefully putting the blade down and putting his knife back in his pocket, Trent walked over and stood beside Ethan as his mom walked in the room.

"The bedroom you guys just finished looks amazing. I have some furnishings ordered, and I'm heading off to an estate sale a couple days from now, hoping to pick up a few pieces that will pull things together. After that, we'll have our first bedroom finished."

"We're making progress," Ethan said.

"Slowly." She held the tray out. "Iva May dropped this off. She wanted to make sure I shared with you guys. Help yourselves. I didn't bring forks up, so hopefully your fingers are okay."

"If it doesn't offend you, I'm good with it," Ethan said. Trent hadn't bothered to answer but had grabbed a couple of pieces as soon as she said it was okay to use his fingers.

"This is looking good," Leiklyn said, looking around. "But I think my July first open date was a little optimistic. Which is too bad, because as rudimentary as the website was that I threw up, I actually have three people booked. That's all the rooms I made available on the website."

"So you're booked for the beginning of July, but you're afraid we won't be ready to open in time?" Ethan said, biting into a crisp apple slice.

"Exactly."

"Do you have the red tape sorted out? There are licenses and in-spections, those kinds of things, that you need anyway. It's not just about getting work done."

"I have all that lined up, and while I don't think anyone is going to do anything underhanded, I've met nothing but positive responses with getting the manor opened up. I know I won't be meeting any road-blocks, as long as we have everything we need." She shrugged. "They even called a special meeting of the council to push our food license through. I have an inspection, but I don't think I'll have any trouble with the kitchen."

"Me either. You're just afraid you won't have three rooms ready?"

"Yeah. I guess. I'm working on the dining room, but I might not get that done either. It's huge, and I didn't realize how much work it was going to be."

"If I get three bedrooms done, I can come down to give you a hand finishing that."

"I appreciate it, although I don't want to pull you from your work. I also was hoping to get a couple of the reading nooks finished and maybe the sunroom. Just...people are gonna come here and have a bed-room and a kitchen done, and I want them to be able to enjoy the house a little bit. Maybe I'm pushing too hard."

"No. That's not too hard. You want them to enjoy it so they come back. That makes sense."

Her look said she was surprised that he would think like that and understand where her concern was.

"Hey, I'm gonna run down and grab a drink, do you want anything, Mr. Ethan?" Trent asked before popping a handful of grapes into his mouth.

"I'm good. Thanks for asking," Ethan said, his eyes flicking to Trent, who was already three quarters of the way to the door, before going back to Leiklyn.

There were dark circles under her eyes. Maybe it was just his imagination, but it seemed like in the week or so since he'd seen her first, she'd lost weight.

"I'm going to stick this tray in the refrigerator, and you can help yourself anytime. We certainly can't eat all of this, so I hope you'll not be shy."

She started to turn to leave, and he found himself wishing she would stay.

"Leiklyn?"

She stopped, standing there for just a moment before she looked over her shoulder, her brows raised. "Yes?"

There were a million things he wanted to say and probably that many more he should. Maybe an apology. Definitely an apology. But more than that, he wanted to know if she still felt drawn to him, like he felt toward her. It never left him. She'd always been the only woman who affected him that way.

But none of that came out.

"I don't want to pry, but I'm afraid you might be working yourself too hard trying to get this done. It won't do anyone any good if you're laid up in the hospital, or dead of exhaustion, even if the house does get finished."

Her eyes frosted over, and he thought for a minute she was going to put him in his place, then her shoulders sagged, and the coldness left her face.

"Thanks. I know you're not saying that to be pushy or unkind."

"No. I'm concerned about you."

"I appreciate it. You're right. I have been pushing pretty hard, and I'm tired."

"You're taking Sunday off though, of course?" he asked, knowing she hadn't taken last Sunday off.

"I wasn't going to. There's so much that needs to be done." She lifted a hand and spread it around as though indicating everything in the room. Grabbing a grape and eating it, she said, "It's just for a month or two. And then I can slow down."

"Tell you what. You go to church with me on Sunday, we'll eat Sunday dinner together, you and Myla and Trent and me, and then I'll help you Sunday afternoon."

"No. I can't have you working on Sunday just because I am."

"You're not having me do anything. I'm bartering with you."

That made her smile. And his word worked. "Bartering?"

"I'm trading Sunday morning for Sunday afternoon, and then I end up getting the whole day with you."

That was too pushy, because she shut down immediately, the humor fleeing her eyes and something that looked a little bit like panic entering them.

"As friends," he said quickly, hoping to diffuse the rejection he knew was coming.

"I'm not sure we can be friends," she said, and that short sentence was laden with so much emotion it drooped under the load.

"I thought we agreed we didn't hate each other?"

"I don't hate you."

"Then we can be friends."

He was pushing her, he knew. But he hated this awkwardness that lay heavy between them. Maybe she would never like him, not the way he knew he would be able to like her, love her even, definitely love her, but he didn't want this almost stranger feeling to push them apart.

"I guess."

"I'll pick you and Myla and Trent up for church on Sunday morning. I'll take care of dinner afterward. And I'll spend the afternoon here, working."

He hadn't been sure how she'd react to his pushing. For some women, he knew it would get their back up and make them fight even harder. But she smiled and seemed to deflate a little as she nodded. "Thanks. We'll plan on it."

Feeling even more daring, or maybe brave, he walked toward her, stopping right beside her, holding her eyes. His hand came up, and he took two slices of apple off the tray.

"Thanks."

He was thanking her not just for the fruit but for agreeing to go to church with him, and he figured she knew it. Her expression didn't change. But two little spots of color appeared on either cheek. One side of her mouth quirked up, and she jerked her head just a little, acknowledging his words, before she turned and hurried quickly out of the room.

It wasn't hard to remember what he liked about her so much when they were younger. Everything was there, only it was so much better, because she had matured and become a beautiful woman. Not necessarily her looks, which were pleasing to him, but he had no idea how to judge that with the world's standards. But on the inside. She was a beautiful woman on the inside. Not perfect, but beautiful.

Chapter 10

Saturday, Leiklyn got up extra early. If she was going to lose tomorrow morning, she wanted to put in some extra hours today.

While she appreciated Ethan taking care of her—when was the last time anyone did that—his request had made her nervous.

Maybe that was the reason she got up. What had she been thinking? Did she really want to show up in church beside him? People were going to think they were together.

She wasn't much of a breakfast person; her kids were old enough to fend for themselves, with eggs in the refrigerator, bread for toast, and cereal if they wanted it in the pantry. So she went into the dining room and got started.

Thankfully, the huge old table had been left by some prior owner, and she'd managed to sand it and finish it last week, making it look better than she'd ever dreamed it could. The floor had already been done, probably Ethan at some point, although she hadn't asked, and the walls looked great as well. She just needed to paint the trim, and the dining room would be done.

Two hours later, she was almost finished when there was a knock at the back kitchen door, and a voice called out, "Leiklyn? Are you in here?"

It was about the time Ethan usually got there, but she'd already heard him come in and go upstairs. Whoever this was, she didn't recognize their voice.

She straightened, a hand on the small of her back, her paintbrush in the other. She walked to the doorway and popped her head around just in time to see a man and a woman walking into the kitchen.

"You must be Leiklyn," the man said.

"I am," she said, responding to the friendly tone of his voice and the smile on the face of the lady with him.

"I'm Adam Coates, and this is my wife, Lindy. Ethan, from the hardware store, said he was working here and there was a pile of stuff to do. Lindy and I aren't experts, but I owned a contracting business for years, and Lindy and I just put an addition on our small beach cottage last fall for our parents to stay in when they visit."

"What he's saying is we're not experts exactly, but we'll help you wherever we can."

Leiklyn just stared at them for a moment. She had Ethan to thank for this. She'd been concerned about whether or not she was going to get it finished, and he'd spread the word in their town. And like most small towns, that was all it took for people to just show up.

"Also, our daughter usually works at our ice-cream shop, but she has the day off to come, and she's making lunch. She should be bringing it in around twelve." The man paused.

"That is, if you can use us?" Lindy said with a smile.

"I can use you. Trust me, I can use you," Leiklyn said, her heart full. "Are you sure you want to spend your Saturday here?"

"Sure am. It'll be just like the old days, back when our business pretty much did anything, and we worked together, before I started specializing in outside work." Their eyes met, and something seemed to pass between them. Their smiles were warm and loving, and for a few seconds, Leiklyn was pretty sure they didn't know she was in the room.

Finally, they shifted and looked back at her.

"Ethan said he was working upstairs. Do you mind if we just mosey on up there and let him put us to work?" Adam asked, obviously used to taking charge and delegating jobs.

"That would be fantastic. I appreciate it," Leiklyn said, loving even that little courtesy that she wouldn't have to quit doing what she was doing to show them around. Ethan was taking care of everything.

"Maybe sometime we can get together and chat," Lindy said as she followed her husband out of the dining room, waving.

"I'd love that," Leiklyn said, returning her wave and watching as she disappeared out of the doorway.

She was interrupted twice more, first as a man who introduced himself as Dr. John and his wife, Anitra, appeared. They had no experience doing anything but painting, and so that's what they said Ethan was going to put them to work doing. They explained that they had a sitter for the kids and that this was like a date for them, so she figured that's probably why Ethan put them in a room by themselves.

An athletic-looking dude and his girlfriend showed up not long after that, and by that time, Leiklyn wasn't even surprised when they said they were there to work and that Ethan had told them she could use the help. She had no idea how she was going to pay all these people back, but she appreciated the help more than she could say.

Lunch was a loud affair as they laughed and joked that the shop fronts in Blueberry Beach were being run by teenagers, since most of the adults who owned the shops had ended up at the inn to help.

When she tried to thank them for all that they had done, John put up his hand. "Your inn is going to draw business for all of us. We're excited about it. Helping it happen this summer is the least we can do."

"I don't want to take business from the diner," she said, knowing that Anitra, John's wife, was the owner.

"The food that you're going to serve is different than what we do. I think we'll complement each other. You definitely won't be taking business from us. We see this as nothing but a positive." Anitra's words eased her mind, and her heart was warmed as she saw Adam and Lindy's daughter, Sierra, talking to Myla. She just caught snatches of their conversation, but it sounded like Sierra was telling Myla how she made the lasagna.

It was delicious and filling. But not so heavy that she didn't feel like she couldn't go right back to work.

As her eyes moved from her daughter, they caught on Ethan who was sitting across the kitchen on a stepladder, since the table wasn't big enough. She had offered to have everyone go to the dining room where she'd been working and sit down, but they declined, since the room would have to be cleaned after they all ate.

His feet were propped on the bottom step, his legs spread, and he held his plate between them. His hands were brown and strong and capable. And he looked better than he did when he was a teenager for sure.

But it wasn't his looks that got her. Not nearly so much as what he had done for her today. He'd brought practically the whole town, and they made her feel like she was a part of it. He'd encouraged her without saying a word. He'd used his actions to show her that he would support her and be behind her. He hadn't just given lip service to something while his actions told a different story.

She'd been around a lot of people like that, and Ethan wasn't one of them.

She needed to thank him. But, as their eyes met, thanking him wasn't what was on her mind.

His eyes, holding humor, and caring, and also a little bit of that same concern that he'd shown when he asked her to take Sunday morning off and go to church with him, made her want to forget that there was laughter and conversation and a whole pile of people in the room beyond them. Meeting his gaze made it all fall away, made her want to walk around the table and stop at his side.

She didn't want to get sucked into that idea again, the idea that she really meant something to someone, when as soon as he "conquered" her, he would be on to his next conquest.

Or whatever it was that her ex had done. Regardless, she could hardly compare the two men. Ethan was in a league of his own. No one had ever done anything this kind for her before.

She made a note that if she didn't see Ethan tonight, she'd be sure to thank him tomorrow when they went to church together.

Chapter 11

That evening after the last car had left, Leiklyn found Myla sitting on the front porch step, her head in her hands, her knees pulled up.

Still basking in a happy glow resulting from watching people she didn't even know help her fix the inn, Leiklyn hadn't figured out how to thank Ethan for organizing everything.

It wasn't even organized. For just spreading the word that she needed help to people he knew would come and lend a hand.

She hadn't considered doing that, wouldn't have done that for herself, and was so very grateful to Ethan that he knew it would work and had made the effort.

Not to mention, her son had had an amazing day.

Week.

Ethan had been excellent with him, patient and kind. And Trent was learning skills he could use for the rest of his life. Not to mention he idolized Ethan. The other men who'd been there today had treated Trent like one of them, and every time she caught a glimpse of her son, he had a smile on his face.

Even Myla seemed to have had a good day, but as Leiklyn slipped out the door and into the dark breeze of the late evening, she wondered if whatever had been bothering Myla lately was something more than just regular teenage angst.

"Mind if I join you?" Leiklyn asked softly.

From the glow of the moon, she could see Myla's head jerk up. She'd been so deep in her thoughts she hadn't heard the door open.

"If you want," she said with a dismissive shrug of her shoulders.

Leiklyn felt like maybe she really wasn't wanted, but she sat down anyway, praying that tonight would be the night that Myla would tell her what was really wrong.

She sat down, tempted to start a conversation immediately but just keeping her mouth closed and her eyes open. A shadow moved in the dark, and she followed it with her eyes. A wild animal?

She squinted, and then she whispered, "Is that a cat?"

Myla nodded. "I've been feeding her out around back after supper since we moved in. She's let me get close enough to touch her, but I haven't been able to pick her up yet."

"You might not want to. If it's a wild animal, it won't have its shots and could bite you and make you sick."

"Mom. I know." Her tone wasn't sarcastic exactly, but there was a hint of exasperation in it.

Leiklyn figured she probably deserved it. It seemed like just yesterday that her children were little and needed to be protected from everything. Being that she was the only parent involved, the responsibility weighed heavily on her to keep them safe.

Now that her daughter was fifteen, she was certainly capable of making rational decisions. And Leiklyn had tried hard to step back and let go.

Sometimes, it was just hard to remember.

"I'm sorry. I know you do. Sometimes, I can't believe how grown-up you are." She put her arms around herself, against the chill of the evening but also against the idea that soon her children would be gone. She loved the idea, and it was liberating in some ways, although it saddened her deeply in more. It was hard to believe when they were little that there would come a day when they would walk out, although from birth, a parent knew that day was inevitable. It just never felt like it would actually come.

"I'm calling her Cheddar," Myla volunteered, and Leiklyn almost fell off the step.

Her daughter had said something on her own that wasn't an answer to a question.

"It's a great name for a cat," she said. "Does it like cheese?"

"Yeah." Myla laughed a little. "That's how I named it."

"I love your heart, that you see a stray and are feeding it."

"She's pregnant," Myla said, not adding anymore.

"That makes it even better."

"I guess I just felt bad for her."

Leiklyn was quiet about that for a moment. And from Myla's tone, it almost sounded like she was saying something more. Something...

Little warning bells started going off in Leiklyn's head. Little thoughts, sentences, pictures in her mind that were streaming together now, and she almost gasped aloud.

Pressing her mouth tightly closed, she kept the words that were in her heart and brain from tripping out.

She didn't want to say anything that would further alienate her daughter.

She would have sworn on a stack of Bibles that she had an excellent relationship with her daughter. That her daughter would tell her anything. That her daughter wouldn't be afraid of her reaction or not tell her something so important.

She pulled back on her thoughts. She was jumping to a lot of conclusions. Although, everything made sense now.

Myla hadn't spoken to her for several months without being asked a question. She got quiet and introspective. She'd been gone a lot before their move, but Leiklyn had chalked it up to them moving and Myla wanting to spend as much time as she could with her friends. Particularly a new friend she had called Jamie.

Leiklyn had assumed it was a girl.

"Jamie is a boy, isn't he?" Leiklyn finally said, unable to find the words and tone that she needed to talk about anything else.

"Yeah," Myla said.

"I didn't know."

"I didn't think you did."

Leiklyn tried to keep her sigh from coming out, and she just blew a silent breath. Her next question, "Are you pregnant?" seemed too blunt. She wanted to ask if Myla was carrying Jamie's child.

But the one thing that she knew she needed to do was to keep Myla from finding out her own secret.

Funny how history repeated itself.

She'd been fifteen as well.

Pregnant.

Ethan had been a boy with character, even if he truly had been a boy. And hadn't yet grown into the honorable man that he became.

"So you and Jamie were together for a while?"

"Yeah," Myla said.

Her daughter sat very still. The shadow that had been moving every once in a while to the side of the walk at the foot of the steps came out as the cat stood at the bottom of the stairs, her head tilted as if listening to the conversation with a vested interest.

"You broke up?"

"Yeah," Myla said.

Maybe that's why she was so quiet. She was heartbroken over breaking up with her first boyfriend. Leiklyn could only hope that was it.

Her gut told her there was more.

"Is there anything else you want to tell me?"

"No. Not really."

"I'm a little disappointed. I thought we'd talk about your first boyfriend together. I guess... I guess you don't have to. But I just thought we had a better relationship than that."

"You wouldn't have approved of him."

Leiklyn wasn't sure what to say about that. If Myla was indeed pregnant, she certainly knew why Leiklyn wouldn't have approved of him.

"So... If you want to be friends with someone your mom doesn't approve of, that's a good reason to hide it from her?" Leiklyn wasn't sure how to show Myla the flaw in the logic of that thinking.

"He liked me, Mom. I wanted to spend time with him because boys don't usually like me. And Jamie did. And I knew you'd tell me no, and then I'd still be dateless and a loser. I wanted to be with a guy who wanted me."

Leiklyn's throat closed up. Maybe she was taking it wrong, but it felt to her like Myla might as well be saying, "Dad didn't want you, and he didn't want me either. And I'm going to jump into the lap of the first man who looks at me and actually says he wants me. Even if he's a liar, and even if he's a jerk, and even if he is someone you don't approve of."

"Sorry," Leiklyn said. She couldn't think of anything else to say. It seemed like it was all her fault. She'd not been able to keep Devon from leaving her for someone else. She'd not been interesting enough. Pretty enough. Whatever enough.

"I know what you say, Mom. You're beautiful, and God knows it, God loves you, and God has someone for you, if you're just willing to wait for him, blah blah blah," Myla said, in a singsong, irritated voice that said she'd heard it all a million times.

It hurt Leiklyn's heart, and she knew she had to be honest. "You know, I say that, and yet I'm sitting here thinking to myself, this is all my fault. I wasn't pretty enough. I wasn't smart enough. I wasn't interesting enough to keep your dad. And maybe if you had a dad who loved you, and wanted you, and hadn't acted like you were disposable, maybe you wouldn't have been as interested in a boy you knew your mom wouldn't approve of. Because the reason I probably would never have approved of him is because he would have reminded me of someone who wouldn't stay. Who would always be looking for that next conquest. Who wouldn't be faithful, or loyal, or have the character to keep his word."

Even as she said it, the words were ringing hollow with herself. She didn't want someone who was staying with her because he was persevering. She wanted someone who stayed with her because he couldn't help but stay. Because he loved her so much he couldn't imagine life without her.

But she supposed that it wasn't enough to live on feelings. She knew it, even as she wanted it. Regardless, none of that would help Myla.

"It's not your fault that Dad left, Mom. Unless there was a problem with all three of us," Myla said, and there was bitterness in her tone.

"There was no problem with any of us. But especially you and Trent. You were children." She'd always tried hard over the years not to bad-mouth her husband, even when it was with the truth.

Even though he had never really stood beside her and helped her with the children. If, and that was a very strong if, he'd ever decided to step up, she wanted the children to respect him and listen to him. Which they wouldn't do if she had talked him down all their lives. They'd feel nothing but hatred for their dad.

And maybe, if they found out that he wasn't as bad as what she said he was... If he changed... She'd turn out to look like the bad one, for bad-mouthing him.

It hadn't been easy over the years, but she managed to keep her mouth shut anyway. Even if she couldn't usually find anything nice to say about him.

"Did you hear me, Mom? It's not your fault," Myla said, and while sometimes Leiklyn wondered if Myla actually really liked her, there was no question that Myla wanted to make sure that she knew that anything Myla did that was messed up wasn't because of her.

"I feel like there's more to the story," Leiklyn finally said, watching as the cat hopped up one step, then stood cautiously looking at them, swishing her tail back and forth, and waiting.

"There is, but you're not going to want to hear it," Myla said, her voice making her sound like a little girl all over again, not the competent teen she had just seemed to be.

"I guess I could tell you a lot of things that you don't want to hear, things I've messed up with, stupid choices I've made. You've lived through some of them. Remember when I thought I could change the toilet myself?" she asked, eliciting a laugh from Myla.

"I remember. You flooded the bathroom. It was disgusting."

"I know. It was. And you lived through it."

"I also learned that if you're going to change a toilet, you need to turn the water off first."

"You know, hearing you say that, it's like common sense. Of course you have to turn the water off before you take a toilet out. I don't know what I was thinking."

"You were thinking you wanted to have someplace to sit when you had to go to the bathroom. Someplace that wasn't already overflowing."

"I guess it was already overflowing, wasn't it?"

"Yeah, and if I remember right, Trent was sick that day, and it was coming out both ends. And for once, he actually made it to the toilet."

"Yep. That's how I remember it too. Sorry about that image. Feeling a little queasy."

"I'm not, although if it were morning, I might be."

Leiklyn's breath hitched. She breathed in and out, shallow breaths, not quite panting, soft and too quiet to be heard in the night as the cat jumped on one more step. Oblivious to the tension in the air.

"You're pregnant."

The words hung, shimmered, stung, hurt.

"Yeah."

Small. Soft. Saying so much. She not only had her first boyfriend without talking to her mom about it, she'd gone well beyond having a boyfriend, sneaking out, doing things she and her mom had talked about and that she'd promised never to do.

"Aren't you going to tell me you told me so? Aren't you going to tell me that if I'd talked to you about him, it would never have happened? Where's my lecture?"

Her words hurt. Leiklyn pulled her arms tighter around herself.

The cat had made it to the step where Myla's feet, bare toes in her flip-flops, sat.

Her tail twitched. She sniffed the air.

"Do I usually give you lectures? Do I usually say I told you so? Is that how our relationship has worked? That I rub things in your face and do my best to make you feel like dirt every time you make a mistake?"

Leiklyn had tried hard not to repeat the mistakes of her own mother. She couldn't remember ever giving her kids a lecture over a simple mistake. Not that this was simple, but it was most definitely a mistake. Not the baby, but the boyfriend and everything he entailed.

"No, I guess not," Myla said, her eyes on the cat. She moved her hand slowly, holding it out for the cat to sniff. "I guess I just thought that's what I deserved. I suppose I was giving you a hard time for doing what you probably should. Which is yell at me, because I was stupid. Because I told Jamie about the baby, and he doesn't want to have anything to do with it. In fact, he told me to get an abortion and told me he'd pay for half of it. That was his solution."

Leiklyn swallowed. Ethan had never said that to her. In fact, when she'd suggested it as an option, he'd argued with her. He wanted to marry her. Whatever that looked like at fifteen.

Even at the time, only fifteen years old, she'd thought that was a terrible idea. But now? How could marrying Ethan at fifteen be any worse than marrying Devon at twenty?

That marriage had only lasted a few years. Would her marriage to Ethan have lasted longer? Would it have been worse? Would she have been more devastated if Ethan walked out than Devon?

She'd always bought into the "wisdom" that a person should wait until they were older to get married, but how old was older? The marriage that she'd entered into at twenty had lasted three years. How could that be any worse than a marriage entered into at fifteen?

Sometimes, the general "wisdom" of the world didn't make too much sense when one examined it from the lens of experience.

"Did you take him up on it?" she asked softly.

"No. Whatever I'm gonna do, I'm doing on my own. He doesn't want me, and he doesn't want my baby. I'm making this decision."

Myla hadn't asked for her advice, but she kinda figured that if Jamie didn't want the responsibility of the baby, it wouldn't be right for Myla to expect any kind of payment for the baby.

Maybe that would be something they'd talk about eventually, maybe not.

"What are you thinking you're going to do?" Leiklyn asked.

"I wanted to talk it over with you, but I didn't know how to start the conversation. You're my mom. Just because I didn't listen to you once doesn't mean that I think I know everything and don't need you anymore." Myla sounded like there were some tears in her voice, although she didn't sniff, and her attention was still focused on the cat.

"Thanks. I appreciate that," Leiklyn said, and there was just a slight touch of sarcasm in her voice, but Myla picked up on it.

"Are you joking? Seriously, Mom? I have this major problem in my life, and you're laughing about it?"

Leiklyn almost smiled to herself. Myla's tone was slightly goofy and very much reminiscent of their relationship up to two months ago: affectionately teasing.

"I'm not allowed to lecture. I'm not allowed to laugh. What's left?"

"You cry?"

Leiklyn laughed.

"I should have known you'd be okay with this. I was so scared and worried, and I knew I'd done things that you had taught me not to, not to mention I had a boyfriend you'd have hated, and you would have seen right away that he was a jerk and a loser, and I thought I knew better, and the one time in my life I snuck around and did something I shouldn't, now I've got some serious consequences to face."

"They are serious. But they're not the end of the world, either. We'll work through this, we'll figure it out, and we'll do the best thing for everyone, including the little one you're carrying."

Chapter 12

"I didn't think I would ever consider getting an abortion." Myla's eyes slipped away, and she looked down at the ground. "Sometimes, I think that would be the best thing though."

"I understand that." Leiklyn took a breath. She didn't want her kids to ever know what she'd done. But maybe her story would help.

But she'd just told Ethan she'd never told anyone, and she was going to be in church tomorrow morning with him.

If she told, Myla would know what a hypocrite she was, and she could hardly ask Myla not to say anything to Ethan.

Although... She could tell the story without naming the father. Yeah, she could do that.

"I'm gonna tell you something that I've never told you before."

"You're in the witness protection program, and someone from the mob is after you?" Myla said immediately, without missing a breath.

"That's close. Real close. But not quite right."

"I knew it. You work for the CIA. Or...you're a communist spy!"

"Now who's being goofy when it's time to be serious?" Leiklyn said, reaching over and bumping Myla's shoulder with her fingers.

The cat stopped brushing her head against Myla's hand and looked at Leiklyn.

"She must have belonged to Mr. Fields. She's definitely not wild like a feral cat would be."

"Maybe we could ask Mr. Ethan when he comes if she has a name. And if he recognizes her."

"I hope they didn't name her, because I like Cheddar."

"Me too. I thought it was a cool name."

"I think it'd be cool to call her kittens little cheeses."

"Seriously, Mom?"

"Hey. I'm easily entertained."

"You gonna tell me? This terrible thing that you did? This thing that you think is going to shock me?"

"I was pregnant at fifteen."

"I'm shocked." Myla's tone had completely changed from one of light teasing to whispered surprise.

There was a very long period of silence other than the distant sound of waves on the shore and the rustle of the wind through the sparse grass that grew along the sand dunes.

"That almost, *almost* sounds like something you'd joke about. But I think you're serious."

"I am. I was pregnant at fifteen."

"So I have a brother or sister somewhere? Do I get to meet them? Have you been in touch with them? You must have given them up for adoption?"

"I had an abortion."

This silence was even longer. It seemed like even the wind was quiet.

Finally, Leiklyn heard her daughter swallow.

"You had an abortion?" she asked, her words laden with disbelief.

"I did. I went to Chicago. It wasn't hard to find a place that would do it without my parents' consent. All they wanted was my money. It hurt. I bled. I felt like I was going to die which really brought home that someone *did* die. And I knew, beyond a shadow of doubt, that I committed murder." It was her turn to swallow past the tightness in her throat. "You live with that for the rest of your life."

Another long silence. Normally, Myla and she could laugh and joke, and if they weren't talking, any silence felt natural. Like they didn't need to constantly be trying to think of something to say to make noise between them.

But this silence was just as pregnant as the cat.

"You'd go back and do it differently?"

"Oh yeah. Definitely. I thought going to school and being pregnant would be terrible. I thought admitting to my friends and my mom what

I had done would be the worst thing that could ever happen to me. I was so wrong."

"You were pregnant in school?"

"No. I was only eight weeks along when I went to Chicago." She carefully kept Ethan out of it, not even mentioning that he'd been there with her.

She'd also told her mom she was staying at a friend's house. Not that her mom really cared too much about her. But it kept the questions down.

She and Ethan had rented a room at a cheap hotel. One that would actually rent to kids their age. Neither one of them had a fake ID or anything like that. They were both straightlaced, "good" kids.

Maybe, considering what she knew she had done, she should have assumed that her daughter would do that and taken steps to prevent the consequences. She thought her daughter was going to be better than she. Make better decisions.

"I know being in school and being pregnant is not life-and-death, but that was one of my biggest problems. I'm going to be at a new school. It's hard enough to meet new friends and try to fit in, but to be pregnant while I do it and the problems that will make...it makes abortion look like a viable alternative. Just like pushing everything under a rock and getting rid of it. It's so tempting."

"I know."

"I guess you do. But...you feel like you murdered someone?"

"For sure. I wake up in cold sweats in the middle of the night. Even now. I'm still ripped up with guilt. I know God has forgiven me. I know that Jesus took my sin, including that one, onto the cross with him. But that doesn't change the fact that I wish I could do it over again. That I know I'm going to step into heaven and see the baby I killed. I know everything will be okay, because there aren't any tears in heaven, but even though I have head knowledge, sometimes my heart still hurts. A lot."

"I had no idea, Mom. That's a pretty big secret. Do you have any other ones?" It was Myla's turn to be a little bit light and ease the heaviness of the conversation.

"I might have one or two. I think that's enough for tonight though, isn't it?"

"It is." By this time, Myla was scratching the cat's ears, and the feline's purring was loud on the porch.

They didn't say anything for a while, with Myla scratching Cheddar and Leiklyn lost in her thoughts. Thoughts like she'd never thought that her abortion might have any good at all in the world. But maybe, if her experience kept her daughter from making the same mistake, maybe there was a little bit of good that would come out of it.

Not that the life that had been lost was worth it, but one life sacrificed to save another might be a little bit of good in something that was so evil she could hardly stand to think about it.

"Mom, I don't know what to do."

Her daughter's voice sounded scared and small. It hurt Leiklyn's heart. She knew exactly how she felt.

Sliding closer, she put her arm around Myla, who immediately laid her head down on Leiklyn's shoulder.

"We'll figure something out. I agree, though, that going to school while pregnant, a new school, trying to make new friends, will be really hard."

"So we could move back?"

"The house is sold. I don't think I can leave in the middle of these renovations, but if that's an option that needs to be on the table, let's make sure it's there."

"Really? You'd consider moving back just because I want to? Just to make me more comfortable?"

"I guess maybe I haven't done a very good job of making sure you know this over the years, but there's really nothing that I wouldn't do for you and Trent. Pretty much every decision that I've made since you guys were born was made with the thought of what was best for you two in mind. I can't believe that wasn't obvious to you."

Leiklyn didn't mean to be condescending or even incredulous, but she couldn't believe that wasn't something they thought about.

"I suppose I can see that," Myla said thoughtfully. "Sometimes, I don't feel that way."

"I think sometimes when parents have to make decisions that kids don't like or don't agree with, they feel like their parents are really mean. It's really hard to see that they're doing it because it's best for them."

"Like when your mom doesn't approve of your boyfriend? It's because your mom wants what's best for you, not because she wants to be mean or keep you from enjoying your life."

"Yeah. Like that."

Leiklyn sent up a silent prayer, thankful that her daughter had seen that without her having to say anything or point it out. It was always so much better when kids could figure things out on their own, with just a little bit of guidance and maybe being pointed in the right direction.

"What am I going to do?" Myla asked again.

That had to have been the question that had been keeping her up at night. That had been keeping her quiet. That she had fixated on for days, weeks even. What was she going to do?

"What are your thoughts?" Leiklyn said, knowing that it wasn't going to satisfy Myla.

"Well, you already know that I considered abortion. Although I think abortion is wrong in theory, but...it just seems like the easiest decision."

"I agree," Leiklyn said, knowing honesty was always the best policy. Abortion would make the current "problem" go away. "It does seem like the decision that's going to take care of everything and make it all go away. Have you thought of anything else?"

"Adoption. But that means I'd have to be pregnant in school." Myla sighed and shifted under Leiklyn's arm. "Is it terrible that I don't want to do that? I guess I'm being vain and self-centered and selfish."

"I guess you could say that. We usually make decisions that benefit us, not the people around us. But maybe that's why fifteen-year-olds aren't meant to be parents. Those are hard decisions to make. It is always hard to make decisions that benefit...people you don't like, or strangers on the street, or even friends, over ourselves. Especially friends who don't seem to make decisions based on the same criteria."

"You always have the wisest things to say, Mom."

"Aren't you offended that I called you selfish?"

"I missed that. Yeah. I guess I am offended." Myla laughed, joking.

"I'm selfish, too. Just so you don't think that I'm singling you out."

"Mom. I don't think you are. I can't think of a single time when you thought of yourself above me."

"I'm sure there have been times, but we're not talking about me right now. What are our other options?"

"There are other options?"

"Sure. You can keep the baby."

"You just called me selfish and immature. I'm not ready to be a mom."

"That's still an option, right?"

"I guess. But it's not one I really want to think about."

"And we already decided we have the option of moving back. That's not really my favorite, but if it's something we have to do, we'll see if we can work it out."

"That one's my favorite. I definitely don't want to be pregnant in a new school."

"What about homeschool for next year?"

"Only weirdos homeschool."

"Have you ever for one minute thought that we actually aren't weird?"

"Sometimes I like to pretend that we aren't."

They laughed a little together. "That's an option that may not be one you want, but it's an option."

"To be honest, I hadn't considered homeschooling. It wouldn't be like you have to homeschool me forever. It would just be until the baby is born, right?"

"Yeah, and when is that going to be?" Leiklyn asked, figuring she probably should have asked that a lot sooner in their conversation.

"November, I think."

"I see. You're not showing much."

"No. Amy, one of my friends at school, had a sister who was pregnant, and no one could tell for the first six months. She said the midwife said that that was because she had such strong abdominal muscles. I don't have six-pack abs, thankfully, but maybe I'm stronger than you think I am."

"Maybe. Actually, I'm sure you are. I think we're all stronger than we think we are, even if it's not a physical strength. It takes a lot of mental toughness to go through what you've been through."

"Yeah."

"I'm guessing Jamie probably wasn't very easy on you when he broke up with you. I'm sure that took some strength."

"I wanted to tell you so bad, but he broke up with me because I told him that I was pregnant. I didn't want that to come out in the conversation. So I felt like I had to hide it."

"I guess I'd appreciate it if you would consider not hiding things from me in the future. You are fifteen, and you're growing up, but...God still made it that you need a mom. As long as I'm here, God has me here for you."

"Thanks. I guess I knew that. I guess it was just hard to remember. Maybe I was panicking, or maybe I hated myself so much I couldn't imagine how anyone else could love me."

Leiklyn squeezed her daughter, her heart equally sad and happy. Sad, because her daughter was going through a difficult trial. Happy, because their relationship seemed to be back on firm footing.

"I will love you, no matter what you do. No matter how bad you think it is, no matter how bad the rest of the world thinks it is. You are my child, and I will always, *always* love you. I might not agree with you. I might not like what you do. We might not see eye to eye on things, but there will always be love. Always."

Chapter 13

Ethan pulled up to the inn early Sunday morning. He told Leiklyn he'd take her to church, but he hadn't told her what time he'd be there to pick her up. He arrived in time to take them for breakfast if they'd like.

It was a gamble on his part. She hadn't even wanted to agree to the church outing, and he had to admit he understood her issue. If they showed up to church together, the town would have them practically married. Small towns were like that.

Not to mention being that this was early in the morning, people would assume they were together. Some would even assume they'd spent the night together.

He thought they'd managed to keep everything under the radar back when they were in high school. Which was saying something for a small town. But it was possible that there were rumors people had heard.

He didn't want her to be the subject of any rumors. He didn't want to do anything that might scare her away.

He loved her perseverance and her determination, and that sweet kindness that she had shown in school.

The decades between had only made her better. Maybe she felt the same about him.

He figured he was probably kidding himself. She needed someone to work on the inn, and he was available.

He pushed those thoughts aside and didn't even really debate with himself, going straight around to the back side of the inn, parking, and walking up, knocking and waiting, trying to keep his swirling stomach down in his abdomen where it belonged and not flying up and wrapping around his heart.

He'd seen a lot of tourists come and go through the years, had met a lot of women.

The only one who ever turned him inside out and made him think about misty mornings with a coffee cup in his hand, standing on his porch, with his arm around the wife that he'd been wrapped up with all night, was Leiklyn.

He wished he hadn't messed things up when he was a teenager. Maybe that would have been his life for the last decade and a half.

"Hey, Mr. Ethan," Trent said as he opened the door.

"Good morning, Trent," he said, glad that after a week of working with him, the boy greeted him with a smile and confidence. He figured after a summer together, Trent would be a man to be reckoned with.

He was a good kid, and Ethan made a note to tell Leiklyn so.

It was a little hard to think about Trent and Myla without wondering about the baby that...he hated to think that they killed, but that was the summary of what they'd done.

Him just as guilty as her, because he hadn't spent one second trying to talk her out of doing what they'd done to create it.

"Mom said to come in. We're just eating breakfast, and you're welcome to sit down with us," Trent said, holding the door open.

"Then I timed my arrival just right. That was the goal. I caught her cooking breakfast, although I was prepared to take everyone out if you'd have me," he said, stepping into the kitchen and hoping he wasn't too dressed down with his dark blue plaid button-down, new jeans, and cowboy boots.

"I think cooking breakfast is the least I can do for you after everything that you've been doing for me." Leiklyn stood at the stove, spatula poised above the skillet with three pancakes sitting in it.

She looked fresh, her cheeks rosy, her face clean, her hair falling around her shoulders in natural waves, a fitted T-shirt and flowing skirt the perfect match for his outfit. But the thing that he loved best was her smile.

That, and maybe the way her eyes lit up, too. She smiled with them, but also looked at him, not exactly like they shared a secret, but like she admired him.

It was a look a man could get used to.

It was a look he could wake up to and turn out the light with at night.

"You look beautiful this morning, Leiklyn."

Yeah. He shouldn't have said that. But her smile grew wider, although her eyes tucked back down to the skillet, and she stared at the pancakes like they were moving.

He didn't care if they were moving or not; he would eat them anyway, if she cooked them.

Movement caught his eye, and he smiled at Myla as she walked in the room. "And you're just as pretty as your mom," he said to her.

It kind of shocked him at the flattery that came off of his lips. Not that Myla wasn't pretty, because she was, it was just that he wasn't typically the kind of guy that went around telling women that they were pretty or beautiful or anything in between.

In fact, he couldn't remember the last time he'd given a lady a compliment.

That just seemed like something that a husband or father or brother would do. He had no sisters, he wasn't a father or a husband, and he didn't go around complimenting other men's wives or kids.

Apparently, when the opportunity arose though, his mouth worked.

Myla's cheeks pinkened, and she murmured a thank you as she walked into the kitchen and said to her mom, "I'm sorry I slept in. What can I do?"

"If you set the table, that'd be great. Four plates. Mr. Ethan said he was eating with us. Although I guess if I had slept in too, it sounds like Mr. Ethan would have taken us out for breakfast."

"A home-cooked meal beats a restaurant meal any day. What can I do to help?" Ethan asked as he went to the sink and washed his hands.

"If you want to finish the pancakes, I was going to make some eggs over easy."

"That actually is my specialty. Will you let me do it?"

"You cook?" she asked, like she hadn't really believed him when he'd said he cooked for his dad.

"I'm good with eggs. I can cook meat. Hamburgers. Not anything fancy, but I don't usually eat fancy stuff anyway. Plain food is good enough for me."

"We don't typically do fancy either. In fact, Sunday mornings is usually the only morning I actually cook breakfast. The rest of the time, we eat cereal or toast, or the kids are always welcome to make their own."

"But we never do, because that's just way too much work in the morning," Trent said with a grin as he opened the refrigerator door and grabbed the butter.

"Thanks for telling me. I guess I won't show up tomorrow morning thinking that I'm going to get fed before work."

"I hope I'm not taking you from your hardware store business." Leiklyn looked up, concern on her brows as he moved behind her. Following him with her eyes.

"No. I checked on things last night after I got home, and it looks like the kid that's working there is doing a great job. He's been with me for a couple of years, and he's been extremely trustworthy. If I didn't have good help, it might be a different story."

He reached down, opening the cupboard she pointed to and grabbing a skillet out.

Trent had already set the eggs on the counter, and Myla was making toast.

"I can't tell you how much I appreciated what you did yesterday," Leiklyn began.

He tried to wave her off. He didn't want a bunch of gratitude. Not words anyway. He wanted more from her than just words. A lot more. Plus, compliments made him uncomfortable.

"I thought we got a lot done. I was happy about that. Also, everyone in town is always willing to help out. It's kind of a thing."

"I know. I remember that. And you can bet the next time someone else needs help, I'll be there."

He laughed. "That's kind of what makes it great. You know? When you see so many people pulling together to help you, it makes you want to do the same for them."

"An upward cycle. That, and it pulls the town together."

"It sure does."

The butter in his skillet had melted, and he cracked the eggs into it.

"You need some chickens out here. If you're going to have a bed-and-breakfast, you need to have some all-natural eggs to serve with it."

The kitchen was quiet for a minute. Everyone stopped moving, and he looked around like maybe he'd said something wrong.

"I've never thought of that," Leiklyn said at last.

"We could have chickens? That'd be really neat. You think we could do that, Mom?" Trent said, sounding excited.

Ethan tried to hide a smile. Trent was going to get an education this summer. Not just in working, but in life.

He supposed that's the way life was for most kids nowadays though. There wasn't too much for them other than sports and electronics.

Although the blueberry farm his dad had grown up on was sold when he was a teenager, he had great memories of visiting it when he was a kid. Those were memories every kid should have.

They expanded a kid's world, not in a global sense but in the sense where they understood where their food came from and how much work it took to produce it.

Not to mention, playing on a farm was just smack-out fun.

"I don't know anything about chickens. Not about raising them, or taking care of them, or...where do you even get them?" Leiklyn said, tilting her head and flipping a pancake. "I've never seen them at the pet store."

"No, I don't think you get them at the pet store," Ethan said with a little grin.

"But there's this really cool thing called the internet, and you can look things up online. And you don't just have to Google it, there's lots of other search engines as well. You can branch out. Try a new search engine, Google something you've never googled before, like where do I find chickens to buy them so I can raise them and get eggs to eat for my own breakfast and for my bed-and-breakfast?"

She laughed, and it was a sound he wanted to hear for the next hundred years. Or thousand. Or eternity.

He didn't know how heaven worked, exactly, but he was pretty sure a lifetime wouldn't be enough to spend with Leiklyn. He'd want to be next to her in eternity too.

Did married couples get their mansions built side by side?

That was a whimsical question. One that normally wouldn't enter his head. It showed him just how far he'd gone.

"I can do that after I'm done cooking pancakes."

"Wait on the toast, Mom, I'm searching it now. Only, I'm going to shorten that a little," Myla said from her spot over by the toaster.

She seemed less quiet this morning and even a little less withdrawn. There was something...something about her, maybe, that seemed like she was coming out of her shell a little.

His eyes met Leiklyn's for just a moment. He supposed there were questions in his. Not that Myla and her emotional state was any of his business, but it was Leiklyn's daughter, and her issues affected Leiklyn's happiness.

Not to mention, Myla seemed like a sweet and kind younger version of her mother.

Actually, he had to admit Trent, Myla, and Leiklyn were the kind of family unit he admired. They were all up and pitching in and talking to each other, and there was no belligerence or angry attitudes.

Not that he expected families to be perfect all the time, but he just really liked the spirit in this home.

"You can order chicks online. Pretty much any time. But looks like there's some special equipment you need," Myla said as her eyes scanned down through the scroll on her phone.

The toast popped up, and she set her phone down.

"I'm sure we can figure it out," Leiklyn said, the tone of her voice saying she was very interested in trying.

"Where would we keep them?" Trent asked, and Leiklyn's head jerked up like she hadn't even gotten to that point in her thought processes yet.

"I don't know," she said, pouring more batter into the skillet. "We have the shed on the property, but it has a lot of Mr. Ethan's tools in it."

She turned toward him, inches separating them, and he lifted his shoulder.

"They're your buildings. I can move my stuff. Or there is the run-down shed at the corner of the property, the one that's falling down. I can see what needs to be salvaged and see if we can turn that into something that would work."

"Do you think it's too far from the house? It must be at least fifty yards."

"I don't think you want them too close to the house, do you? Not to be graphic, but where there's chickens, there's going to be chicken poop." Ethan grinned as Leiklyn's eyes widened and understanding dawned across her face.

"No. That probably wouldn't be very impressive for the guests to see as soon as they set foot on the property."

"Or smell," Ethan added, and they grinned together.

Maybe their eyes got caught for just a bit. His did, anyway. Thinking about how nice it was to have a woman who smiled at him. He enjoyed a little laughter, a little joke, a little sweetness and fun. He'd been around marriages like that, and he was envious of that type of relationship.

Of course, he'd been around marriages that were almost the exact opposite and been in a couple relationships that had degenerated to that point. Where he wasn't sure what mood the lady was going to be in that day and whether or not it was going to be smiles at breakfast or stony silence.

So far, he'd seen Leiklyn handling the stress of everything having to do with the inn with a calm pleasantness that was refreshing and attractive.

Of course, it wouldn't just be attractive to him. It would be attractive to any single man in her vicinity.

The thought dimmed his happiness just a bit, and he realized that they'd been staring at each other.

He also realized that, from the corner of his eye, he could see Trent was staring at them staring at each other.

The kid wasn't dumb. He was going to know exactly how Ethan felt about his mother.

"We need a fence," Myla said from the toaster, holding her phone again. "Although you can let them run around. They stay pretty well. The fence is for predators, mostly."

"I think that would be really fun. Having chickens dotting the yard and watching them."

"I think I would enjoy that."

"I think you're right. Although most people come here for the views of the lake, I think the chickens would be a nice touch. I wonder if the winters are too cold for them?" Ethan said thoughtfully. Gently putting the spatula under the eggs in the pan, he flipped them carefully.

He loved his eggs over easy, and so did his dad. This wasn't the first time he'd made them in this kitchen.

"I think that's something for us to talk about this afternoon. Although, we need to get the inn up and running and actually have guests before we need to think about chickens laying eggs for breakfast to feed the guests," Leiklyn said, her tone brisk and businesslike.

"The eggs are ready," Ethan said, scooping them up and putting them on the serving plate that Trent had set beside the stove.

"They look better than Mom's," Trent said, with all of the delicacy of a teenage boy.

"Her pancakes look better than mine. Actually, I've never made pancakes, so however they turn out, they're better than anything I've ever made," Ethan said, not wanting Leiklyn to feel bad. Sometimes, kids could be inconsiderate. He'd worked with more than one teenage boy in the years he'd owned the hardware store. Not to mention he'd been one himself, although that point in his life was looking further and further behind him.

"It's okay. Eggs over easy is something I've never mastered. I always break them when I turn them over."

"They're harder than you think, but there is kind of a knack to it. It took me a while, but it's one of my dad's favorite breakfasts, something that's not too hard."

"I'm impressed. They look good," Leiklyn said, eyeing the plate, then putting the last pancake on her plate and turning the skillet off, sliding it to a cool burner.

He liked that too. She didn't need to have the compliments for herself. She wasn't the slightest bit upset that her son had basically called her eggs over easy a disaster.

In his experience, some of the women he'd been around had been supersensitive and easily upset. Pouting when they weren't the center of attention or turning an accidental slight into a major insult and punishing everyone with silence and anger.

He probably had to stop spending all this time thinking about how perfect Leiklyn was. He was here. He was taking her and her family to church, spending the afternoon with them, but that didn't mean she wanted anything more than someone to help her get her inn ready. He needed to remember that. He had a tendency to want to think that he was here in her kitchen today, courting.

He was pretty sure Leiklyn would be surprised to know he was thinking along those lines.

Chapter 14

Church wasn't as awkward as what she was afraid it would be.

She'd honestly been kind of concerned that Ethan was going to parade her up to the front, and she'd have the entire congregation staring at the back of her head the entire time.

That hadn't happened, thankfully.

They hadn't sat in the front, but he hadn't kept her in the back either. She felt comfortable in a pew about halfway up.

Maybe it was where he usually sat, or maybe he was trying to figure out what would put her the most at ease.

After what Ethan had been doing all week—inviting people to come help or spreading the word, making sure Trent felt needed and was learning, and complimenting her daughter—it wouldn't surprise her if he'd chosen the seat solely for her comfort.

What would it be like to be married to a man who actually thought of someone other than himself?

She didn't want to be too hard on her ex. She had been young and immature as well. Not that people who were young and immature couldn't stay married. Couldn't learn to think of each other. Couldn't make vows and keep them.

A person didn't have to be a middle-aged adult or older before they were able to keep their word. Do what was right. Persevere through hard times.

Although, to be fair, it did take some people longer to grow up than others.

Still, without talking bad about her ex, she felt like Ethan would have been that kind of man from the beginning. Not that she thought it would have been a good idea for them to get married. The idea of her own daughter getting married at fifteen made her heart want to skid to a stop.

Still, whether or not a marriage lasted was more about the character of the people in it than the age they were when it began.

In her opinion. But, really, what did she know? She had a failed marriage behind her and little else to show any success.

As they stood in line to walk out, her shoulder brushed Ethan's, and she was tempted to push her arm just that much farther and let their hands brush as well.

Silly temptation.

Remembering the pastor's sermon about forgiveness and not just forgiving other people but forgiving yourself, she almost laughed. He could have been looking into her life this past week as Ethan walked into it and brought up all the old guilt and shame. The pastor could have read that sermon on forgiving yourself just for her.

She supposed God knew what she needed. And that was what she needed today. The payment for sin had been paid. Even though God was holy and couldn't stand sin, he didn't see it anymore because it was covered by the blood of Christ.

She knew that. Had knowledge. Sometimes, it was hard to get head knowledge down to her heart and apply it to her life.

Myla and Trent were walking in front of them, chatting about chickens. Leiklyn had a smile at that.

Ethan had opened a new world to them with one simple statement this morning over breakfast.

She wouldn't mind being married to a man who opened up new worlds to her.

Someone who talked to her. Someone who laughed with her.

"They were together in high school."

Leiklyn almost yanked her head around to see who was talking behind her. It was a whisper, and she figured she wasn't meant to hear.

"I remember. She was such a goody-goody, but I heard some things about them that would shock the world."

"You're kidding? I never heard anything."

"Well, I did. Although my mom forced me not to say anything, because she said it was probably gossip but—"

The voice was cut off when a little kid yelled, "Mommy! Mommy! I have to go potty."

Tempted to turn around, Leiklyn managed to resist that urge, but she did move her head slightly to look at the man beside her.

He'd heard too. She could see it in his face as he looked down at her.

There was probably worry on her own, creases of care and concern.

Ethan's face darkened, and his eyes flickered as he leaned toward her, bending down. "I'd like to talk to you a little bit this afternoon. Could we?"

She didn't want to. He'd want to talk about the very thing that she never wanted to mention again. Not in her life. But, she supposed, if it was going to come out—and that was an if—they might not have been talking about Ethan and her at all. They might have been talking about someone completely different, but she couldn't be scared to death every time the idea came up that people might find out what she'd done. She had to grow up and face it. Part of that was talking to the man who'd been with her when it happened.

She nodded. "Once I feed the kids and dinner is over, we'll make the time."

His lips turned up, not to smile necessarily, just acknowledging what she'd said as he nodded. His eyes still held hers, and the concern that poured out of them made her knees weak.

Maybe this was the way he made everyone he was with feel. Like they were the only people in the world. Like he was more concerned about their comfort and welfare than anything else. Like he wanted to make sure he treated them right, and that he would ease their way if possible.

Maybe he did make everyone feel like that, but she couldn't help feeling special. Because she was beside him. Not because she had nowhere else to be, not because she'd asked, but because he'd asked her.

Chapter 15

Leiklyn didn't look at Ethan as they moved with the crowd toward the exit where the pastor was shaking hands.

"This pastor is new here," Ethan said casually, maybe trying to turn the subject of her thoughts.

"I thought his message was excellent," Leiklyn replied, trying to put the words she'd just heard behind her and will her hands to quit sweating and her heart to quit pumping in her throat.

They could have been talking about anyone.

"Everyone loved him when he was a candidate, although he's unmarried and some people thought that would be a stumbling block."

"Why?"

"He's not that old, probably our age. People thought he might be more interested in getting a wife than pastoring a church. But he's been pretty serious about his calling, about shepherding the flock. Plus, I've never listened to a message of his that didn't convict me somehow."

"If today's message was any indication, I believe that."

Someone jostled her in the crowd, but she didn't turn to look. The back of her hand brushed Ethan's, and she couldn't snatch it away fast enough. She didn't want her name linked with his, not that she was embarrassed to be seen with him, but the words she'd just heard still rang in her ears and she wanted that part of her past to stay buried. Deep.

"Don't let what they said bother you," Ethan said, leaning his head down so his words fell directly in her ear.

"Is it that obvious?" she asked, tilting her head, knowing they probably looked like they were whispering to each other, which they were, and it wasn't really something that normal people did walking out of church.

Still, there was a little tightening around his eyes, and she thought that maybe she hurt his feelings when she jerked away.

"It's not you."

"I know. It's you." His smile was thin.

"It's not. It's just the idea. I don't want anyone to know." She said the last sentence barely loud enough for him to catch her words.

"Would it be so terrible if people knew?"

She held his eyes for just a second, thinking about last night and telling Myla. Myla hadn't judged her, and she'd taken it better than she thought. Actually, it almost worked out for good. Maybe. At least Leiklyn could tell her honestly how it felt and what a person had to live with after they had done what she had.

"It's a small town. You know how hard that can be."

"I'll stand with you. It's not like you're going to have to face this with the scarlet letter slapped on your chest all by yourself. I'm not leaving you. She was my child, too."

"She?"

"Did you ever think she was anything else?"

She hadn't.

She lifted her brows and a shoulder and then looked away. They'd moved to the point where her eyes landed on the preacher and his outstretched hand.

"Pastor, this is Leiklyn. She recently moved into the Indigo Inn. She's going to be opening it soon," Ethan said by way of introduction as he shook the pastor's hand.

"That's fantastic. I hated to see that big old building just wasting away out on the beach. It will be a great thing for this town. If you have a lobby, we can put some tracts from the church in it."

Leiklyn had to smile as she grasped his outstretched hand. He wasn't letting any grass grow under his feet. And was serious about his job, just as Ethan had said.

"Of course. You're welcome to put tracts anywhere you want to."

"And Bibles in all the rooms," the pastor said with a smile and a lifted brow.

She appreciated that he wasn't pushing her. "Of course. Not all the rooms are finished."

The pastor nodded. "I heard Ethan was out there helping you. I also heard a rumor that it would be opening sometime in July. Is that close?" he asked, seeming like he had all day to talk to them.

She liked that he wasn't in a hurry, that they got his full attention, and even though he didn't know her, the caring and concern in his eyes couldn't be faked.

The man obviously was living his calling.

"I hope so. I think we're gonna make it, but only because Ethan talked to people from town and they've come to help out. I don't know what I would do without them."

"That's what a small town's for. That's what the church is for, too. If there's anything we can do, let us know. I'm sure the ladies would be happy to provide a meal if you have a town-wide workday out there. I'm not much good with electricity. It tends to get away from me and set things on fire, if you know what I mean, but I know how to use a hammer and drill, and I'm not afraid to get dirty."

Leiklyn giggled a little at the idea of the pastor setting things on fire. "I didn't even know the last one was happening. Ethan just told people, and they started showing up. It shocked me, but I appreciated it."

"Make sure you let me know about the next one, okay, Ethan?"

"Yes, sir. Although, I don't want you to take too much time away from your sermon prep. It was a good one today."

"I agree," Leiklyn said. "It was exactly what I needed to hear. Thank you."

"Forgiveness is a hard subject. Glad you appreciated it." The pastor smiled at them again, and they moved on.

Chapter 16

Dinner was a subdued affair, although Trent and Myla chattered about chickens. Ethan chimed in with an occasional comment. Apparently, he'd had some experience with them when he was a teenager on his grandfather's farm. Which she hadn't known about and hadn't realized was somewhere around here. It had been sold when he was a teen, he said, and she hadn't realized that either.

Funny how she could have spent so much time with someone and not known such a basic thing about him.

But her mind was not on chickens, it was on her daughter, who seemed to be like a typical youth and resilient. Maybe just talking to her mom about her situation had eased the burden from her shoulders, but her whole demeanor seemed to be much lighter today, and she was more chatty than she had been in a very long time.

Not back to her normal self, but better.

They just had sandwiches, so there wasn't much cleanup to do, although Ethan helped with it like he'd helped with the breakfast dishes.

Devon had never helped her with anything in the kitchen or related to housework or children. In fact, if she wanted to go somewhere or do something, she had to ask him to babysit like he wasn't even the father. Maybe that's the way all men were, but she had a hard time imagining that Ethan would have been like that.

Regardless, Ethan was drying the last dish when he said, "Leiklyn, would you like to take a walk?"

She felt her son's eyes move to her, and she held her breath for just a couple of seconds, thinking that he was going to want to jump in and go along, but then his eyes seemed to move from her to Ethan and back to her again, and he said, "Yesterday, Ethan told me a couple things I could do if I had time and wanted to. So I'm going to run upstairs and work on that closet some more." He threw the napkins into the garbage can and brushed his hands together.

"You don't have to work. It's Sunday," Leiklyn said, thankful he hadn't asked to go along but feeling bad that he was going to go work instead.

"I've really been enjoying this. It's not like work to me. I guess I'm still in the fun stage of it."

"I never got out of that stage either," Ethan said. "Although, walking on the beach with a beautiful woman does beat drywalling any day." He hesitated, then his eyes went to Leiklyn's. "Not just any beautiful woman."

Her heart was doing cartwheels, and her stomach twirled in a slow flip, making everything inside of her feel off-kilter and wobbly.

His words were just the kind of words that a girl always wanted to hear, but they didn't seem to be uttered with casual ease or practiced flattery. They seemed sincere, like he was just saying what he really felt and not what he had told a million girls before.

Something about being with him made her feel special. She would have sworn she was too old and mature to care about that kind of feeling, but she found that wasn't true. She liked feeling like she was special, the only one, but, like he had just said, she didn't think it would mean as much with just any man.

It was Ethan she wanted to be the only one for.

"I'm gonna go see if I can find Cheddar and give her some leftovers. Maybe she's had her kittens." Myla glanced out the window. "I hope she finds someplace that will be dry if it rains."

"Cats are usually pretty good at that," Ethan said.

"Oh! We wanted to ask if your father had had a cat here."

"There was a stray that came around sometimes. She was orange and white spotted."

"I think that's Cheddar! Maybe if we see her outside, you can tell us."

"Sure. And if she needs a little place to have her kittens, maybe I can whip something up tonight and bring it tomorrow morning. How soon will she be going to have them?"

Myla shrugged. "I have no idea." Her eyes shone. "Would you really make something? I never even considered that. I just know she can't be inside. The inspector said no animals in the house."

"I would. It would be my pleasure. I do that kind of thing on the side."

"Work with wood?" Leiklyn asked, curious despite herself. What was it that made her want to know everything about him?

"Yeah. I guess if I hadn't been a woodworker, I'd have been a farmer, but from what I remember, a farmer does a lot of working with wood, as well as other things. Seems like there's always something to fix, something that's broke down, something you need to do with your hands."

Leiklyn nodded. "You'd have made a great farmer. You've got that salt-of-the-earth steadiness about you that someone who works land needs to have."

Her words pleased him, if the working up of his lips was any indication. Plus, she liked that twinkle in his eye. She liked when they were serious and concerned and focused on her, but she liked the lighter parts of him too. Liked to see that he was smiling and happy and that it was because of her.

"You never said if you wanted to take a walk?"

"Yes," Leiklyn said, this time with no hesitation.

"Thanks." He gave her a look that said maybe despite what they talked about in church, he wasn't sure whether she would change her mind. The idea made her sad, like he couldn't depend on her to make a decision and stick with it. Or to keep her word. Maybe it was just her imagination, because as far as she knew, she'd never lied to him. Lying was something she tried hard not to do at any time.

He opened the door for her. She finished drying her hands on the dish towel and hung it up before stepping out into the beautiful late spring afternoon.

"I always thought the best time to walk on the beach was in the morning, with the mist over the waters and the sand. Makes it feel a little mysterious and romantic."

"Romantic?" She lifted her brow, looking over at him as they walked around the inn together and picked their way down the sandy path toward the beach.

"What? You didn't think I could be romantic?"

"It just doesn't seem like something you'd admire. Or maybe men in general. But I didn't mean it as an insult. I just thought it was kind of a funny thing for you to point out."

"Maybe you just bring out the romantic in me."

She wanted to. She wanted the romantic in him to come out when she was around and not for anyone else, but at their ages, it seemed a little silly.

"I actually haven't walked on the beach in the morning since I've come. But I know what you mean. There's typically a breeze during the day and no mist, but especially in the spring, you get those misty mornings that are gorgeous."

"And romantic."

"And romantic," she said.

Chapter 17

They didn't say anything more as they walked down the path, through the dunes, and out onto the beach.

"Looks like we're not the only ones that had this idea," Leiklyn said as they saw people spread out all up and down the beach.

"It's a beautiful day. What better thing to do in Blueberry Beach on Sunday afternoon than take a walk on the shore?"

"I suppose that's true. The lake is beautiful to look at and so relaxing."

"If you don't want to be seen with me, we can go back." Ethan tried to keep the hurt out of his voice. He'd been very aware in church when their hands brushed, and she yanked hers away. It had been right after they'd heard people talking about what could have been them, although it might not have been. In his experience, it was always a bad idea to make assumptions, especially about gossip.

Still, he respected the fact that Leiklyn was still trying to work through her past and didn't necessarily want to be linked with him.

"No."

He liked the way her chin came out. He also liked the narrowed look in her eyes, like she was determined to push through. Whether or not that meant she was pushing through because she was stubborn, or because she liked him, he wasn't sure.

"You sure?"

"I'm sorry for my knee-jerk reaction in the church. It was wrong of me. If I could go back and do it again, I would do it differently. It's not fair of me to punish you for something I feel guilty about."

"I feel guilty about it too."

Her head turned, and her eyes widened, like she could hardly believe what he just said.

"You have nothing to feel guilty about. It was my body. My choice."

"Really? I had nothing to do with it?"

She stared at him. He could almost see his words rolling around in her head. "I never blamed you. Not in any way."

"Could have fooled me. I'm pretty sure after we got back home from the trip to Chicago, you didn't talk to me again for eighteen years. In the few times we ran into each other, you couldn't get away from me fast enough."

Her head hung down, and it twisted his heart. He hadn't meant to make her feel bad. She already felt guilty about the baby. She didn't have to feel guilty about blaming him as well.

"I didn't blame you, honest. It's just...seeing you made me feel even more guilty. It brought everything back."

"I don't know what you were going through, but I know I was hurting. You turning away from me made it so much worse. Like, like it was all my fault. Like your pain was all my fault."

"That's not the way it was! I just couldn't stand to see you, because it brought back all the memories but also because you knew. You knew how terrible I was. You knew that I'd committed murder. No one else knew that I had done something so egregiously awful." She shook her head, kicking the sand as they walked. "I figured you probably couldn't stand to look at me. You had to hate me."

He couldn't believe she felt that way. He'd been certain she hated *him*. "Never. I wish you'd have talked to me about it, because that's not the slightest bit true. None of that is the way I felt. I didn't hate you, and while I didn't admire what we'd done, I definitely didn't think less of you about it. And yes, *us*. I was there too."

"You tried to talk me out of it."

"Not that hard. And I came up with half the money."

"You would have paid for it all."

"Right. I *would* have paid for it all. You were taking care of my 'problem' too. Not saying our baby was a problem. I'm just saying you weren't the only one benefiting from that decision. I wasn't in any position to have a wife, support a baby, do anything to help you. So, yeah, I put up a token resistance because abortion seems so wrong, but I was also secretly relieved that was what we were doing, because I had no idea how to do anything else."

She had stopped walking while he was talking and stared at him, her face a mixture of her pain and disbelief, before she seemed to begin to understand what he was saying. "I didn't know."

"You wouldn't let me tell you."

"I didn't want to change my mind. I knew what we were doing was wrong, but I didn't want to do anything else. Everything else was going to be harder."

"I know. I felt the same."

"I'm sorry I didn't give you a chance to tell me that."

They hadn't fought. They hadn't argued. They hadn't really even talked about it much at all. Although he did remember asking her not to have an abortion, it hadn't been the main thing he'd said. Funny she would remember that after all these years.

"You didn't hate me," she finally whispered.

"Never. I never hated you. I wanted to be with you." He couldn't stand looking in her eyes anymore, so he blew out a breath and looked across the horizon where water met sky. "It probably wouldn't have worked out. We were too young. Whether we kept the baby or whether we gave it up for adoption, I don't know that 'us' would have worked out. Fifteen is so young."

"I know. There were times I wondered that too."

"Wondered what?" He turned back to her, his head tilted.

"Whether a relationship with you would have lasted any longer than my relationship with the man I eventually married at twenty."

"It didn't last long?" He had heard it had been a short marriage, but he supposed he wanted the words from her.

"No. Trent wasn't even walking when we split."

"Sorry." That had to have been hard too. "I guess you've done a lot of hard things."

"It was for the best." She lifted a shoulder and shook her head. "I shouldn't have married him."

"He was abusive?" Ethan's fingers curled. He wasn't sure he could stand here and listen to her tell him that someone had hit her.

"No. He left me, cheated. But he never hit me. That's not what I meant." Her tongue came out, and she ran it along her upper lip before shoving her hands into her pockets and looking at him. "I meant I just thought it was best for me to marry someone that I wasn't so blindly attracted to. After all, no one could match what I felt for you, but more than that, I thought about what we'd done together, and I didn't want to have those feelings for anyone else, those feelings that would make me do things I never thought I would. To make me lose control, I guess."

Ethan wasn't sure what to say. She was admitting that she didn't love her husband the way she'd loved him, but it didn't sound like she felt like that was a good thing.

"Funny." She laughed without humor. "Because I ended up completely losing control anyway. Not with my feelings, but I certainly didn't want my husband to leave me to raise two small children by myself. Not to mention I loved him in a way. It was devastating when he left."

"I bet. With two little ones and everything being your responsibility."

"Yeah. I suppose when your spouse leaves, especially for someone else, it takes your confidence along with it. It just makes you feel worthless. Like there's something wrong with you when you can't keep your spouse, can't keep your marriage, or can't be enough."

He blew out a breath, his hands fisting again. Her ex hadn't hit her, but he dealt emotional blows that were probably just as bad, if not worse. "You've been through so much, and all I can think is that I wish I could have been there to go through all that with you. Even if you just wanted me as a friend."

She shook her head, laughing a little. "I don't feel like I could ever be your friend."

That hurt. A lot. It took all his words away. Maybe it would have helped if he could have been angry. If he could lash out and try to hurt her the way she'd hurt him. But he could never react like that. He loved her then. He loved her now. Love wouldn't let him hurt her.

He swallowed past the tightness in his chest and shoved his hands in his pockets, turning away from her. Not saying anything, because there wasn't anything for him to say.

He wanted to be her friend. For the rest of her life, he wanted to be her friend. And more.

"I'm sorry. I said that badly, too, didn't I?"

"You're just saying the truth," he said, his words sounding normal which shocked him, since he felt anything but normal.

"It's the truth, but I think maybe you took it the wrong way."

What other way was there to take it? He clamped his jaw tight and turned his head, but not his body, to look at her, his brows raised, but no words.

"Were you listening to me?" she asked, a little exasperation in her voice but also affection. He was pretty sure that was affection.

"I hurt you."

"I said that the blind attraction I felt for you, still feel for you, was too strong." She tilted her head. "That's why I could never be just friends with you. I would always want more."

So, yeah. His mouth was hanging open. "I guess the subject has slowly been changing, and I'm having trouble twisting with it."

"I'm sorry. You're right. We started off talking about the abortion."

"That I helped pay for. That I took you to. I didn't try to talk you out of. It was our child. Our abortion." He wanted her to get that, if nothing else.

"Thank you. I guess the guilt is a little lighter if it's shared."

"Yes. I don't think it's something that I'll ever be completely free of, but I don't want to live in the past either."

He wanted to get back to what she'd said about attraction, but he supposed it was probably better to work through this first, and then he could ask her exactly what she meant about that whole attraction thing and not wanting to be friends. It wasn't what he thought, but... Could it be what he hoped?

"Me either. When we were in school, seeing you brought everything back. It made me feel guilty." Her steps slowed as she spoke thoughtfully. "Now, being with you has been making me feel like it's okay to put it away. That the one night, the thing that we did, doesn't define me. It's not something that I would do now, and it's not something that I would do again if I had a chance to go back and do it over."

"Me either. For sure." He shifted, turning to face her. "We were fifteen. Too stupid to make any kind of good decision."

"I know. You're right." Her mouth opened, then closed, then it opened again. "I admitted to Myla last night that I've had an abortion." She put a hand up, as though to stop him, and maybe it was reflex, maybe it was deliberate, but his hand came up and took a hold of hers, cradling it in his, covering it with his other hand.

Her eyes dropped down to their hands as his cradled hers, and she continued.

"I didn't mention you. She doesn't know who the father was. I didn't want to tell her without asking you if it was okay. And it was a spur-of-the-moment thing in a conversation that we were having. But it made me realize that, first of all, it wasn't such a hard thing to admit. And I know I had a bad reaction in church today, but looking back, maybe hiding it isn't the best course of action. I can't really help other people if they don't know that I've gone through it too, can I?"

"That's true."

"And I also realize that I might be able to help other people with my story, sharing the years of guilt and regret."

"That's a good point. And, just for the record, any time you want to talk to anyone about it, you can mention me. I was there too. It's not my proudest moment, by far, but we did it together. I'm not afraid to stand with you on it. I want to. You weren't alone, and I can shoulder my share of the blame."

"Thank you," she whispered.

Her hand, soft and worn, different than he remembered, more mature, nails not painted but short, beautiful because it was hers, lay cradled in his, and he didn't want to push to end the conversation, but her hand in his made him want to revisit what she'd said before.

"Can I ask you something?" he finally asked.

"Of course."

"You said you didn't want to be my friend."

"I said I couldn't be your friend."

He hoped the subtle difference in wording meant what he thought it did. "But you also said you were attracted to me."

She ducked her head, and maybe her cheeks were a little pink.

"I'm not sure where that leaves us."

"I'm sorry. I didn't mean to make you uncomfortable, if you're over us."

"I never got over you." His words came out harsher than he intended, but only because he meant them from his very soul.

Her eyes lifted, and they stopped walking, staring at each other. He saw disbelief cross her face and then a little smile.

"Really?" she asked, and there was so much more than that one word.

"I dated. I had a couple of long relationships too. Enough that I felt like maybe I could never duplicate young love, and I would never find what we had. I thought about settling, but I think the ladies I was with knew I wasn't as into them as I should have been, and they always ended up breaking things off."

"That's probably what I should have done too, except I wouldn't have had my children. And I don't regret them at all."

"They're good kids. I love the relationship you have with them. You're the adult, and they respect you, but there's obviously affection in your relationship that runs both ways."

"Thanks. I can't take credit for it. We have a good relationship because they're good kids."

"Or you have a good relationship because you're a good woman."

"Do..." Her hand turned in his, and slowly, as though she were waiting for him to pull away and ready to allow it if he wanted, her hand slid against his until their fingers threaded together. "Do you want to try again?" she asked softly.

His heart beat against his chest, and his lungs labored. He tried to make his voice sound normal. "More than anything. It's what I wanted since I first stood on the step of the inn and saw you in the door and realized who you are. It's all I've been able to think about." His free hand came up and brushed against her cheek as he squeezed her hand with his. "I want to be with you, but I think we got a little out of line last time, and I don't want that to happen again. I think it's best to go slow."

She smiled a little. "I'm not getting any younger. How slow are we talking?"

He laughed. She'd broken the serious spell that had been weaving its way into his soul. Where he wanted to start spouting poetry, telling her all the pretty words, all the words he didn't have. He didn't have poetry. He just had honesty. Hopefully, it would be enough.

"I don't know. Long enough for you to be sure you can put up with me, I guess."

She lifted her brows, because his answer was a non-answer.

What was he even thinking exactly? Why did he want to go slow? She was waiting for an answer, and he was wondering exactly how slow "slow" was. A month?

"You've got a lot on your plate right now with getting the inn open. How about we wait until after opening."

She let out an exaggerated sigh of relief. "I thought you were talking decades. I thought you were really going to test me and be sure I was gonna stick this time."

"You didn't not stick last time."

"If it weren't for me, we might still be together."

"We don't know. Maybe we'd have done something stupid... There's no point trying to relive the past. It's over."

"That's right... So, we're friends, but we're not going to stay friends for long?" Leiklyn asked.

"We're holding-hands friends. And no. I don't think that stage will last long at all."

"That's a relief." Her eyes crinkled and she smiled at him, and although he could still see lurking sadness behind the glint of humor, he felt like taking the time to talk to each other, really talk to each other, had been even more profitable than what he thought it would be.

He certainly hadn't thought when he started the day that he would end it holding her hand.

Chapter 18

Leiklyn walked along the beach, holding Ethan's hand and smiling to herself. Probably she shouldn't be smiling. Probably she should be kicking herself for all the wasted years when they hadn't really talked. At least, it'd only taken one week after meeting again to clear the air between them.

She could point the blame for all of those years right at herself. She was the one who had turned away. She was the one who had decided not to include him in her life. It was all her fault.

Funny how it was so easy to see it now, but at the time, she thought she was doing the absolute best thing for herself.

"I'm not trying to start our first fight, but...you look tired to me, and I wish you'd slow down a little. Let me shoulder a little more of the burden of getting the inn ready so you can slack off a bit."

Ethan's thumb rubbed over her hand, comforting and familiar, even though she hadn't held his hand in decades.

Maybe it was the tone of voice he used, or maybe it was that skin-on-skin contact. The contact that said he cared about her and wanted the best for her.

Whatever it was, his words, far from making her angry, made her feel loved and cherished.

"I bought the inn for a dollar right before we graduated from high school. Actually, we closed on it after we graduated. Tiffany and Willan and I all have our names on the deed. When we met at the beginning of April, Tiffany was going to foot most of the bill for the renovations, and Willan has money she was going to invest as well. I didn't have a job. I didn't have money. All I have are my kids and a willingness to work. That's why I'm the one here. I feel like I need to earn my keep, since I'm not investing any money into it."

"I see. I wondered how that all went down."

"The idea was originally mine. I talked to someone at a wedding of all places, and things just worked out. It was the right price anyway."

"I can hardly imagine it being sold for a dollar."

"Normally, when a house is repossessed because of unpaid fines, the person who buys it has to pay the fines. But the man I talked to at the wedding said that the council just wanted to unload the property to someone, anyone who would make sure to keep it up, and fast, since they didn't want to be saddled with it over the tourist season. I just came along at the right time, talking to the right person."

"Funny how so much of life is like that. Where the right thing happens at the right time."

"Funny. Or just the Lord working things out."

"Yeah. That's it." Beside her, Ethan sighed a little and then looked over. "I understand what you're saying, but...I care about you. Obviously." He held out their joined hands, like he wouldn't be walking on the beach holding hands with someone he didn't care about. Of course he wouldn't be. Ethan wasn't that kind of man. "I'd like to see you at least take a little bit of time off. You're there before I am in the morning, and you're there after I leave. It was all I could do to get you to take a little bit of time off today."

She appreciated that he was concerned about her. It made her feel like he truly cared about her. She also appreciated that he wasn't commanding her but asking kindly. It made her want to do whatever he wanted.

"I'm meeting with Tiffany and Willan at the diner on Friday. I'll take the whole morning off. Will that work?"

"That's a good start. Thank you."

"I'm taking today off, and Friday morning. That's more than I had planned to take off."

"You should be taking a nap rather than taking a walk on the beach then, if this is your day off."

The only thing that would make a nap more appealing than walking on the beach with Ethan would be if Ethan were napping with her. But considering that they were taking things slow, she supposed that wasn't in her near future. She also supposed it wasn't something she should say aloud.

"I'd rather be walking with you," she murmured, managing to keep everything else to herself.

She hadn't really been paying attention to where they were going or to the other people on the beach, so she was a little surprised to look up and see people she recognized walking toward them.

"They were at the inn yesterday, weren't they?" she asked, nodding her head at the couple holding hands while laughing and walking toward them. They were flanked on either side by three teenaged girls.

"That's right. That's Dwane and Laura."

"They look pretty happy for as long as they must have been married," she said, eyeing the girls who were late teens at least.

"Actually, they're not married yet. I think I heard a rumor that Dwane proposed and Laura accepted, but they haven't set a date because Dwane's mother-in-law has pancreatic cancer and isn't expected to make it through the month." Ethan's voice dipped a little on that last bit.

Leiklyn tilted her head in acknowledgment of his words.

They made her think.

Life was short. It was also uncertain.

"It's good to know that I'm not the only one who's getting a late start finding the man of her dreams."

"The man of your dreams? Really?" Ethan asked, and although there was a little tease in his voice, he was serious.

"Is that too cheesy?" she asked with a little smile.

"No. Not at all. It's just not enough. I like compliments, coming from you, anyway."

"Then I'll have to make sure I give them to you," she said, and their eyes met for just a second before they both looked ahead, smiling in greeting at the couple in front of them.

"It's good to see you guys around. I've been hearing you're putting a lot of long hours into fixing up the inn," Dwane said as they stopped in front of each other.

"Funny you should mention it. I was just trying to talk Leiklyn into slowing down a little. It's a little embarrassing when the lady can out-work you." Ethan had a lot of tease and no seriousness in his tone, and Leiklyn laughed.

"I hardly think I'm outworking him. He just doesn't live at the inn, and I do."

"It's beautiful," Laura said. "I'd never been in it before, and I was so excited when we were able to come and help. Not that I only came so I could nose around the inn and see how gorgeous it was, but..."

"You need to be honest, Laura," Dwane said with a twinkle in his eye. He turned back to Ethan and Leiklyn and said in a stage whisper, "She only came so she could see the inside of the inn."

Laura elbowed Dwane in the side, and he grunted like it truly hurt, even though Leiklyn could see she barely touched him.

"How's your mother-in-law?" Ethan asked, watching as the girls grouped themselves together closer to the edge of the lake and took a selfie. They weren't in hearing distance, and Leiklyn was glad as Dwane spoke.

"Not well. Hospice is in, and they're focused on keeping the pain down and making sure she's comfortable."

"That's sad," Leiklyn said.

"It is, but it's also good in a way. The Lord worked everything out so that we were able to get Lizzie before Dawn got really bad. And that's a real blessing," Laura said, her voice subdued, her eyes on her girls.

"And Laura's grandfather seems to have taken a shine to her. I don't think his interest is necessarily romantic, but they seem to have a lot of interests in common, and he's been able to brighten her remaining days. It's really neat the way everything worked out," Dwane said, dropping Laura's hand as she leaned into him and putting his arm around her, squeezing her to him.

"That's true," Laura agreed.

"I thought I heard you two were looking at buying a house," Ethan said.

Leiklyn was tempted to tease him about the hardware store being a hotbed of gossip. She had no idea he knew so much about what was going on in the town.

Dwane and Laura smiled at each other. A special smile that held secrets and knowledge—the smile of lovers everywhere. "I asked the lady to marry me, and she said she would. I figured I ought to at least offer her a house to live in rather than take her to my apartment that is even more cramped than hers is."

"I don't mind a cramped apartment as long as we're together."

"That's what she's supposed to say," Dwane said with a wink.

"That's what I mean," she said, her eyes adoring on her husband-to-be.

"When's the big day?"

"We're thinking it's going to be soon. We thought Dawn would like to know that we're settled and Lizzie has a permanent home with us."

"I'm sure that will ease her mind. It seems like people like to have things settled before they pass on," Ethan said, surprising Leiklyn with his insight.

"That's true. We're hoping she holds out so that we can show her the house we're buying. We don't close on that for two weeks though, so we're not sure how that's going to play out."

"If she takes a turn for the worse, we'll get married before we have a house. But if she holds out, we'll wait until we close."

"I love that," Leiklyn said. "Sometimes, people are so concerned about making their wedding just perfect for themselves, and it's all about them. It's so refreshing to see people who are more concerned about making their day about everyone. What a nice change."

She was guilty of the same. Her wedding had been a huge affair; she hadn't considered anyone but herself, what she wanted, and what her husband wanted. It seemed selfish now, looking back on it.

On her wedding day, they were already getting each other. Why would they want anything more?

"We'd better keep on going, I promised Leiklyn that if she took a little time off, I'd work with her on the inn this afternoon. She's definitely taken some time off for me, so I suppose I ought to put some time in working for her."

"It's a give-and-take, that's for sure," Dwane said as they moved away, smiling and promising to come if they had another workday.

"I'm sure you've already thought of this," Ethan mused, "but the inn would be an excellent place to have weddings."

"I suppose the thought has gone through my head, but I also think I've been so focused on trying to get it open that I haven't had a chance to think about it."

"Our wedding could be the first wedding at the inn after its grand reopening."

"Are you asking me to marry you?"

"No, I didn't come prepared to do that today. But I suppose it won't be a shock to you to know that's coming. That's what I want anyway."

"I guess I won't be surprised then when it happens."

"I guess not." He paused as though thinking about saying something more. But in the end, he said, "Are you ready to head back? We can get some work done, although I'm fine if you want to take some more time off."

"I will. Take time off, that is. On Friday, remember?"

"I'm not sure that meeting with your friends about your inn is considered time off."

"We're eating at the diner. Surely that counts for something."

"I guess if you're not cooking. That can count for a little anyway," he said, tugging on her hand and turning around with her.

She smiled, swinging their hands between them, closing her eyes to the breeze that blew across her face. The lake scent, the sunshine, the sand between her toes, and a good man beside her. She almost felt like her life was finally falling into place.

Chapter 19

By Thursday night, Ethan felt like the week had been four years long rather than four days.

Everything that could go wrong had.

There had been a leak in the new bedroom that Trent and he had just finished, and the water had managed to not only completely destroy the bedroom and bath that was leaking, but the water seeped under the floor overnight on Tuesday night and completely ruined the subfloor of the adjoining bedroom as well.

Wednesday had been spent in damage control and cleanup, and on Thursday, it felt like he was back to square one.

Leiklyn was always working by the time he arrived in the morning, no matter how early he showed up, but he didn't leave until she had quit for the night. No matter how late it was.

Thursday was no different, and after starting at four, Leiklyn finally put her head in the bedroom that he and Trent had not quite managed to finish and said, "Let's call it a day."

"I thought you'd never say that," he said from the stepladder where he was spackling in the corner of the ceiling.

Exhausted and barely able to stay on his feet, Trent had reluctantly quit a half hour earlier when Ethan had sent him away.

"I think I might have to push the open date back. Which is going to kill me because we have people booked."

"I think if you try to open on time, it's going to kill you," he said, coming down from the ladder and grabbing the lid for the spackling.

She didn't even argue with him, she was so tired.

"Did you eat something?" he asked. Myla had brought some sandwiches up a few hours before for Trent and him, and they'd stopped work long enough to eat them, washing them down with a bottle of water. He hadn't gone looking for Leiklyn.

"I did. Do you have a minute to sit outside on the porch steps with me? I have something I want to tell you."

His stomach immediately cramped.

They hadn't seen each other much all week. Leiklyn had been busy dealing with the fallout from each catastrophe while he'd been busy cleaning up the mess.

She didn't seem upset. She didn't seem like she'd changed her mind and wanted to break up with him.

He wasn't sure why his mind went there, but it did.

Maybe because it was his biggest fear.

It almost seemed too good to be true that they were finally together. He didn't want to do anything to jeopardize them this time.

He wouldn't be with Leiklyn if he didn't think she'd stick with him. But he supposed, since she was the one to break it off years ago, that was a legitimate fear.

"I have to close the lid on this spackling, and then I'll be down."

"Thanks. Myla made some cookies. I'll bring some out."

"Pretty sure you just said the word that will make me do things in half the time."

"Cookies?"

"That's right. Especially if they were just baked."

"She made them after supper. They're probably still warm."

"Pretty tempted to just ditch the spackling and run down the stairs. But I suppose that would be too much like a teenage boy?"

"I think it's okay for your inner teenager to come out sometimes. You were pretty mature as a teenager anyway."

She didn't seem like she was about to give him his walking papers, and he had deliberately kept his words light, trying not to let his fear show.

It wasn't even five minutes later when he stepped out on the porch to see her leaning against the front post, staring at the water.

It was dark, just a small glow from the stars overhead shone on the rippling waves. And despite the calendar that said summer was here, it was chilly.

"That breeze feels good after being inside all day."

"Smells good too. I don't think there's any place in the world that smells better than Blueberry Beach."

"Your opinion might be a little biased, but you have lived more places than I have, so I'll believe you."

Leiklyn laughed. "I hope I didn't scare you, but I was talking to my daughter today, and there was something that I really wanted to tell you when we were talking on Sunday but I didn't have permission. I do now, and I wanted you to know."

"Okay."

"I know it's not going to change anything, but...Myla's pregnant."

He supposed laughter was a stress relief. Sometimes when he got a shock or even sad news, a person felt like laughing just to let the stress out.

Now, he wanted to laugh just because it felt so crazily ironic. "She's the same age as you were?"

"Yes. Only the father doesn't have the character you did."

"It didn't take much character to pay for half an abortion."

"You stood by me. Even if it was a terrible decision, we made it together. And if I'd wanted to keep her, I think it would have made you happy."

"It would have."

"He broke up with her and offered to pay for half the abortion when she told him."

"Then I guess I have something in common with him."

"I don't think so. Nothing in fact. Anyway, I hope she's not going to choose to terminate the pregnancy, but she isn't sure. She's thinking she might keep her or give her up for adoption."

"You know it's a girl?" he asked, feeling like it was a little thing they could smile over. Since both of them had decided their baby had been a girl.

"She doesn't know. I just found out this week. Actually Saturday. You know how this week has been. But we need to make appointments and start to make plans for the future."

"What can I do?"

"You're already doing everything you possibly can."

"I want to do more."

She turned, closing the step between them, and wrapping her arms around his waist, and leaning her head on his chest. He didn't hesitate to enfold her in his arms and put his nose down on her hair, breathing deeply. Her scent had matured along with the rest of her, and he loved it better than the teenage bubblegum and strawberries she used to smell like.

"Okay. I guess I wanted this too."

"Someone to hold you?"

"Not someone. You." She sighed. "Being a single mom is so hard."

"I don't know how to be a dad, but I'm here to stand beside you, so you don't have to do it alone."

"I've longed for that so much. Thank you."

They stood on the porch for a while, with Ethan just holding her and her quiet in his arms.

"I didn't have any right to be upset with her."

"I can't imagine that you would be even if you did feel like you have the right."

"It's a mistake. Not the baby, just the actions. You're right. I couldn't get upset about that. But remember how we were talking about maybe what we had done being something that could be turned into good because I had the experience and I could tell people how it feels? How the guilt never leaves? How I will always wonder what might have been, and how I feel like a murderer?"

"I remember."

"I wanted to tell you then that when Myla told me she was thinking about having an abortion, I was able to tell her what I've been living with all my life. She wasn't set on the idea anyway, and I think it might change her mind. So, not that I think that what we did was a good thing, but I do think that something good might come out of it."

"I see. And I agree. God can use our mistakes for our good and His glory. Sometimes, it doesn't feel that way, and sometimes, it takes a long time for things to turn around."

"Exactly."

"Thanks for telling me."

"Thank you for wanting to know. For being willing to do whatever I need and whatever will help me."

Ethan didn't say anything but tightened his arms around her. He'd been thinking about kissing her all week, just hadn't had the opportunity. Maybe the opportunity was now, but it didn't seem like the right time.

"Oh! I forgot about the cookies."

"It's okay. I'll grab one before I walk out. I'd rather hold you anyway."

"Holding me is better than eating cookies?" she asked with humor lacing her tone.

"That's pretty big, isn't it?" he said, allowing humor in his own voice.

"It sure is. It tells me I'm pretty important to you."

"That you are, Leiklyn. That you are."

Chapter 20

Friday morning, Leiklyn grabbed her purse on her way out of the kitchen. She had had plans to get up and get a couple of hours of work in before she had to go, but Ethan had probably been right. She was so tired she could barely get out of bed in time to meet her friends, let alone get up early and do extra work.

Ethan had said she was pushing herself too hard and needed a break. He was probably right.

But after the week she'd had, she didn't feel like she had much of a choice. She hated going into the meeting she had planned with Tiffany and Willan and admitting how little they had accomplished.

Mostly because Ethan was working as hard as he could.

Jumping on social media to upload her latest pictures, she took a few minutes to respond to some of the interaction, glad it was popular. She even had people asking when the inn would be open. Maybe she'd actually book a few people from her social media posts. That would be neat.

Her phone buzzed with a text, and she glanced down. Ethan. She smiled as she clicked on the message.

I forgot to tell you there are some people coming tomorrow to help.

That would be wonderful! But I hate for people to give up another Saturday.

I didn't ask anyone to help. I just had four or five guys texting me telling me they were coming. So don't feel like we're putting anyone out.

Thanks for telling me. I don't want to become a pain.

I think they're happy to know there's a job to do and it's something they can help with.

Good point. She knew she was. Sometimes, she wanted to help, but she didn't know what to do or would be helpful.

Have a good time with your friends.

She smiled, probably a goofy, silly, romantic smile that she should have outgrown years ago.

Thanks.

She tried to school her features into something a little bit more mature as she tossed her phone in her purse, taking one last glance around the kitchen before she walked out the back door.

Her steps slowed as the door shut behind her and her eyes landed on Myla, hunched down at the side of the steps and petting Cheddar.

The box that Ethan had made sat in a corner on the porch, empty.

Cheddar, heavily pregnant, rubbed her head against Myla's hand and purred loudly.

"Hasn't she had those babies yet?"

Myla's head turned, then she slowly straightened. "Mom?"

"Yes?" Leiklyn asked, trepidation filling her chest. Just the tone in that one word made her shiver and brace herself.

"I've decided I want an abortion."

Leiklyn tried not to gasp and look dismayed, although that was how she felt. She didn't want to put Myla off from talking to her because of her terrible reaction. "I see. I thought you were leaning in a different direction? Did something happen to change your mind?"

"I announced yesterday on social media that I was pregnant, and...I had to delete my account. I can't go to school and face that every day." As she turned, Leiklyn could see her eyes had dark circles under them and were red from crying.

"Oh, honey," Leiklyn said, dropping her purse on the porch and going down the stairs with her arms open. Why did her child's pain always hurt her so terribly?

Her heart bled for her baby. For the pain and the struggle. Neither of which were over yet. In fact, Leiklyn could almost say with assurance that it was just the beginning.

As soon as Myla's head hit her chest, she started to sob. Leiklyn just held her tight—there was nothing else she could do.

Leiklyn had already said everything she could. Now she just had to decide how much dictating she could do in her fifteen-year-old's life.

It was one thing to make her eat spinach and go to bed at a decent hour. It was quite another to force her to go through a pregnancy she didn't want. But could she allow her to commit murder?

She didn't know.

"Mom, I'm so sorry. Sorry that's not what you want me to do. Sorry that I'm in this position." She gasped for air. "Sometimes, I hate this baby."

Leiklyn could understand all of that. There were times she had hated her baby, too. It had caused such a huge disruption in her life. It wasn't hard to resent it and want it gone.

It had been a long time since she'd gone through this, but she should have expected the change of mind, mood swings, and, most of all, the reactions of her peers.

"Honey, please don't blame yourself. I know I've always said you need to take responsibility for your actions, so I'm not saying that you shouldn't in this case."

"I know." Myla sniffed.

"But I should have kept a better eye on you. You never lied to me or did anything that was remotely wrong. And I trusted you. Which I don't regret, but even adults need someone to keep them accountable. I do. I know that, and I should have been keeping you accountable as well. I didn't do what I should have done as your mother. That's where the problem is."

"You're the best mom in the world. It's not your fault that I didn't want to hear what you had to say. And snuck around behind your back."

"I guess we're a pair, aren't we? Both of us want to take the blame."

Her daughter sniffled out a little laugh, but it didn't hold much humor.

"I don't want to kill my baby, but..." She sighed and snuggled closer to her mom. "The decision just seems so hard. Why does it have to be so hard?"

Leiklyn could go through all of her usual comments. That life is hard. That hard things make her stronger. That right decisions build character. That struggle makes her better. But she just didn't feel like that was what Myla needed right now.

"It is hard. And I understand that. And I'm here. I just want you to know that, so you understand you don't have to go through this by yourself. Okay?"

"Thanks." Myla took a deep, trembling breath. "I felt so much better since I talked to you. I guess I need to talk about it, which is probably why I stupidly announced on social media yesterday that I was pregnant. It was a dumb decision." She reached a hand up and wiped a tear off her chin. "I wasn't expecting the rash of comments. I mean, I thought there might be a few people who might be like, oh, that's terrible, but I thought most of my friends from my old school would be supportive if not happy. But everybody's telling me I'm too young and I need to get rid of it. A couple even told me that they'd help me sneak behind your back to do that."

"That's what I did. To this day, my mom doesn't know what I did." She hadn't even thought about it until just now. She probably should call her mom and tell her so she didn't find out from someone else.

She and her mom didn't have a close relationship and usually only talked on the phone once or twice a month. If that.

In fact, it had been a month since she'd talked to her, and she hadn't even told her that she was moving back to Blueberry Beach. Not that her mom would care.

So many things to feel guilty about. She was a terrible mom, a terrible daughter, and a terrible friend.

"Are you going to hate me for getting an abortion?" her daughter whispered with her head still on her chest.

"I will never hate you. No matter what you do." She wanted to add that she thought it was a bad idea or that she thought Myla could make a better decision, but Myla already knew that.

Still, her heart broke at the idea that her daughter was even considering it.

Could she really stand back and allow her to do that?

So many times as she'd raised her children, she'd wished that she had someone to talk to about things. To make decisions with. To help decide what was right.

This was one of those times.

Ethan would help. Ethan would listen. Her head and her heart were in agreement on that. But part of her pulled back from the idea. Maybe she was afraid of needing him too much. Or maybe she just wasn't used to not being alone.

Obviously, killing someone was wrong. Dead wrong. But how old did her child have to be before Leiklyn, as her parent, needed to step back and allow her to make her own moral decisions?

She could tell her she could have an abortion but she had to move out of her house. Or she could force her to not have an abortion and make her carry the baby to term, even if she gave it up.

Neither one of those things were decisions she wanted to make. Neither one of them seemed like the best thing for her daughter. Maybe, maybe she just needed to stand back and let her daughter think about it and pray that she would make the decision that was morally right, even if it was a hard decision.

One thing Leiklyn knew for sure. She couldn't judge her if she didn't. After all, she made the same stupid decision, thinking that it was the fastest and easiest way to get rid of the problem.

"Mom, I know you have to go. I don't want to keep you. I just... I just wanted to tell you what I had decided."

"I see. I appreciate it. I hate to leave when you're so obviously upset."

"I'll be okay. I just know that no decision I make is going to be a good one. The time for making a good decision is already gone."

They talked a little bit more, with Myla assuring her that she was fine, before Leiklyn finally got her purse and drove to the Blueberry Café on Main Street in Blueberry Beach.

Iva May was at the cash register when she walked in, and by the furrowed brows and concern in her kindly blue eyes, she knew something was wrong. But Leiklyn was late. She could see Tiffany and Willan already sitting at the table.

The diner was busy, too.

Iva May just said, "I'll be praying for you," after she'd rung her up and Leiklyn paid.

Leiklyn appreciated it, knew she meant what she said. It made her feel good to know that someone else was praying. Hopefully, it would help Myla to make the right decision.

She grabbed her drink and walked over to the table where her friends sat.

"Hey, Tiffany. Willan," she greeted them as she reached the table and went to sit down opposite them.

Tiffany snapped her head around and stood immediately. "Oh my goodness! You had such a rough week."

"I didn't even put all of it on social media," Leiklyn said, figuring she might as well get the worst news out immediately as Tiffany's arms came around her and she squeezed.

Willan stood as well and hugged her as soon as Tiffany's arms dropped. "I hadn't been following much on social media, but Tiffany was telling me all about it. It sounds like a terrible week. I wish I could be there to help."

"I feel like I'm doing my part by being here. I just feel terrible because we were hoping that we would start getting some income from it, and I don't have any money to put into it, so the sooner it can start generating its own, the better."

"About that," Tiffany said, biting her lip, sliding back into her seat, and picking up her straw paper, twisting it in her hands.

After her discussion with her daughter, Leiklyn would have said nothing else could upset her, but her heart shivered and her chest felt painful.

From Tiffany's tone, this could be nothing but bad news.

"Is there a problem?" Willan asked, lines between her brows, the concern in her eyes showing she had picked up on the same hints Leiklyn had.

"I didn't want to break it quite like this. I thought maybe we'd talk a little first. But I also don't want you to be under any illusions. I found out late last night that my ex is fighting the divorce settlement, which was supposed to be final next week. He's claiming I cheated on him and left and he shouldn't have to pay me anything. Lies. All of it. But I thought the money was in the bag. It's not."

Tiffany's face scrunched up, and her eyes filled.

Leiklyn put her hand over top of Tiffany's. Willan did the same to her other hand, and they both squeezed.

"I don't know how far along you are on the repairs. Or I guess I should say I don't know how deeply you're in debt and expecting me to pay. But the money I said I was going to have was supposed to come from that. Everything was supposed to be settled, but he hired a new lawyer and got a judge to go along with him." Her head dropped. "I feel terrible."

"Don't. You can't do anything about it, and it wasn't your fault," Leiklyn said, automatically almost, since part of her mind was whirling.

Ethan hadn't been paid for anything that he'd been doing. But she knew for a fact that he'd been paying Trent, because she'd just gone with her son yesterday over lunch to open up a checking account in town.

He'd proudly deposited his first paycheck which Ethan had given him that morning.

It was only two weeks' worth of work, but there were also one thousand dollars or more of supplies which she'd purchased solely from his shop.

Actually, she hadn't purchased them. She'd put them on her account which he'd opened for her because she'd assured him Tiffany was coming through with the money.

Would this put Ethan out of business?

Chapter 21

Leiklyn wanted to put her head on the table and sigh, maybe cry a little, but she didn't want Tiffany to know how upset she was.

Not angry upset, but worried upset, and not even worried about herself necessarily, although she'd been planning on the opening of the inn to take over the job that she'd lost. Her unemployment benefits were running out at the end of the month.

"I've ruined everything. I'm sorry," Tiffany said, her fingers squeezing Leiklyn's hand. "I shouldn't have counted my chickens before they hatched. I just thought it was a sure thing."

"Leiklyn said it was fine, and I agree with her. It's not your fault." Willan spoke compassionately.

"We were just talking about how our lives had not worked out the way we thought they were going to. I thought we were all going to go in a new direction. And what could be more fun than working with your friends and owning an inn on a gorgeous lakeshore? I've screwed everything up again. It's the story of my life."

They sat there for a bit, holding each other's hands and letting Tiffany's words sit in the air around them.

What a change it was from the Tiffany of high school who could pretty much do anything she wanted, everything she touched turned to gold, and she was always happy and bubbly and full of optimism.

It stunk the way life beat a person down sometimes.

"We're working to change the story," Leiklyn said.

Maybe it was her tone, because her words were simple, but both of her friends looked at her with wide eyes.

Finally, Tiffany whispered, "How?"

"We're going to figure that out right now. The three of us. Maybe we do have some tragedy in our background. Some mistakes. Some things we wish we hadn't done. But that all equals up to a lot of experience between the three of us, a lot of wisdom we've gained. Surely we

139

can put that experience and wisdom to work for us and make the next eighteen years the best eighteen years of our lives."

Leiklyn wasn't sure where those words were coming from. She felt about as defeated and dejected as Tiffany looked. She hadn't even told her friends about her conversation with her daughter this morning, and she probably wouldn't. Even if Myla had announced her pregnancy on social media, she obviously regretted doing it, and Leiklyn hadn't thought to ask her where she was going from here with that information.

Plus, even if she did think that it was okay to say anything, this was hardly the time.

"Do you really believe that? Are you just saying that to get us all positive thinking or whatever?" Willan asked.

"I believe it. Lots of other people climbed out of pits deeper than the one we're in. We can do it too. Because it's not just one of us doing it, it's the three of us." She hesitated for just a second, and then she said, "And Ethan is helping us. I know he'll be on board as well."

"Ethan?" Tiffany said, her head tilting and her eyes, still red, narrowing with thoughtfulness. "The Ethan that you couldn't stand in high school and wouldn't tell us why?"

"Yeah. That Ethan."

"I knew it. I knew you guys had a thing for each other still. That's why you wouldn't talk about him."

"No." Leiklyn drew the word out, not really wanting to change the subject but seeing this as a good opportunity to come clean. "I really do want to talk about the inn and what we're going to do, but...you know Ethan and I were together in high school."

They both nodded while she continued.

"I got pregnant."

Her friends gasped, complete shock showing on their faces as she'd known it would. They'd had no idea.

"I had an abortion."

The shock had not left their faces. If anything, it had grown worse, with both of their jaws dropping. Tiffany's grip on her hand tightened with dawning realization.

The moments ticked off between them while Leiklyn held her breath.

They had every right to be upset with her. It was a huge thing for her to keep from her friends. And now to have dropped it like the bombshell it was was inconsiderate at the very least.

She'd allowed them to think for years that as friends they'd shared everything. But she really hadn't. It was to her detriment too, since her friends had always supported her. Maybe if she'd told them. Maybe if she'd had that kind of courage, she would have found they rallied around her and gave her the courage she needed to go through the pregnancy.

Maybe if she had been more open about exactly what she and Ethan were doing, they would have encouraged her to do right and there wouldn't have been a baby to think about in the first place.

"I can't believe you didn't tell us," Tiffany said, her eyes holding understanding but also hurt.

"I get it," Willan said softly. "We weren't always as supportive as we could have been. Sure, you were probably afraid of what our reaction would be even though we were great friends. Plus, that's a really hard thing." She swallowed and looked down. "Maybe you're right to not say anything. Even now, it makes me a little bit angry to think that there was a baby that nobody wanted and you killed it." She looked up quickly. "Not to kick you. Not now. But... I've longed for a baby for so long. Even if I can't find a man who wants to spend the rest of his life with me, if I had children or at least a family, I'd have a chance to do better with them than my parents did with me." She took a breath, shaking her head a little and looking away. "I'm sorry. I just wanted to say I understand. I feel like a terrible friend."

"No! You were a great friend then and now. I was just so ashamed. It had nothing to do with how I thought you guys would react. It was all about me being ashamed and scared. Maybe if I'd been braver..."

"We can't change the past. We can't make ourselves be different than what we were. But we can make ourselves be different than what we are. Just like you said, right now we can make the decision to be different." Tiffany had kind of taken the lecture that Leiklyn had given and turned it on its head, giving it right back to her. "You were right. It's funny how there's so much room for improvement in my life." Her tone held a fair amount of sarcasm.

"Mine too," Willan said, her tone still subdued.

Leiklyn hadn't realized how Willan had longed for a child. Of course not. They'd lost touch, and Willan hadn't mentioned anything the last time they'd gotten together nor in their short previous conversations.

"I'm so glad you told us. I know that probably took more courage now than it might have even back then, since we don't know each other as well. But I appreciate it. It makes everything make sense now."

"Thanks. I knew I could trust you guys. Not like it's a secret or anything, but I just knew that you both would understand. And I can't really talk about Ethan and why I wouldn't talk to him without mentioning it—"

"You told us about getting pregnant and having an abortion...wait. Why did you quit talking to Ethan and hate him so much? Did he get mad and break up with you because of it?" Willan asked.

Leiklyn realized she hadn't really explained anything but had gotten sidetracked over her guilt and shame.

"No. Ethan was perfect. It was all me. Every time I looked at him, I remembered the terrible thing we had done. He paid for half of it, and he claims he didn't try to talk me out of it, but that's not the way I remember it. I remember he didn't approve and didn't want to do it, but he wouldn't let me do it by myself."

"Wow. What a great guy. Are there any more men like that on planet Earth anywhere?" Tiffany asked, sounding more like her old self than she had in all the interactions that Leiklyn had had with her so far.

"I know, right? So hard to find. I didn't appreciate it because I was just as dumb as a box of rocks."

"I think we all were at that age. Sometimes, I think I still am," Tiffany said with a self-depreciating grin.

Iva May arrived with their food, and she chatted with them for a few minutes before she left. Willan asked the blessing, and they started eating before they resumed talking.

"So you quit talking to Ethan because he reminded you of all the bad things you had done and made you feel ashamed?" Willan finally asked.

Leiklyn nodded. "Pretty much. I guess I just couldn't imagine anyone loving me after what I'd done. After knowing what I had done. I could hardly love myself. I certainly didn't like myself. I felt like no one could find out or they wouldn't like me either."

Her friends nodded, and they ate for a bit in silence. Leiklyn felt so much better now that everything was out in the open. Funny how she'd been so afraid of people's reactions, and she had never considered how much better she would feel when she got it off her chest and didn't have a terrible secret that she was hiding from the rest of the world anymore.

Not that it assuaged the guilt she still felt.

"So, Ethan and you...have been talking to each other all of this time?" Tiffany asked.

"No. He came to the inn to deliver stuff I had ordered from the hardware store, not realizing he owned it. And that's when we met for the first time since high school."

"That wasn't that long ago."

"No. I guess... I guess there's just always been something about Ethan for me. He just feels right. Being with him feels right. Talking to him feels natural. There is no struggle to speak or to understand. We just... Being with him feels like I've been with him forever. If that makes sense."

"Of course it makes sense. You're saying he's a good kisser." Tiffany smirked then put a fry in her mouth.

Leiklyn could feel her cheeks getting red, but she figured she might as well be honest. "In high school, I thought he was. Of course, I didn't have much experience."

"What about now?" Willan asked, her brows drawn together like she was concerned. "You certainly have more experience now since you have two children."

"You just pointed out it's only been a couple of weeks."

"So he hasn't kissed you yet?" Tiffany said, dipping a fry in ketchup.

"No." Leiklyn shrugged, unsure what to say. She would not mind it if he had, but she understood. "He said we should take it slow this time. We went a little too fast when we were in high school."

"So the spark's still there," Willan said.

"It is. Maybe stronger this time. Not the teenage angst, but something deeper. I'm not even sure what. Or how to describe it."

"He was gorgeous in high school," Tiffany said, wiggling her brows.

"...I like the way he looks, I can't deny that. But it's more about the pull he has. It just feels deeper. Maybe that's because I want it to. I don't know."

"No. I think that's possible. I've heard other people talk like that. I've never experienced it though," Tiffany said, sounding more introspective than she had.

"I hope it's true. Like a soulmate, only...not quite so mystic," Willan said, and she almost sounded dreamy.

"Yeah. I don't know. Maybe it will work out this time, maybe it won't." Leiklyn sure hoped it did. "But whatever, we need to figure out what we're going to do about Indigo Inn. We can work to make this work, right? Or are we going to give up now that things didn't quite turn out the way we were expecting?"

"We definitely need to dig in and make it work," Tiffany said thoughtfully. "But we might be more on a time crunch and definitely more on a budget. I do have some money that I can use, and I can sell that fancy car I'm driving. It's paid for."

"I don't need to be paid. I wasn't expecting or intending to pay myself for any work I did on it. Although once my unemployment runs out, I'm going to need to do something to at least buy groceries and necessities for the kids." Leiklyn tapped her finger on her ice water.

"I can pull out of my 401(k)," Willan said.

"No. I don't want you to mess with your retirement. You may need it." Leiklyn felt like she was giving wise advice to her friend, but Willan shook her head.

"Do you have a 401(k)?"

"No."

"Why should I have one? I'll have to look into it and see what I can do."

They talked some more, strategizing ways to come up with money and customers, and it was several hours later before they finally stood up for Leiklyn to take them back to Indigo Inn to give them a tour.

There were so many unknowns in her life, and Leiklyn wasn't sure what to expect. But she did know one thing for certain—she loved being reunited with her friends, and whether this was a success or failure, the fact that they'd revived their friendship made it worth everything in her book.

One more thing she knew was that as long as Ethan was going to stand beside her, she would let him.

Chapter 22

It'd been two weeks since Leiklyn had met with her friends and told Ethan that she wasn't sure whether they were going to be able to financially support the opening of the inn, but they were going to do their best to scrounge up what they could from anywhere they could. She had wanted to warn him that the gig might not be as long term as what she'd originally thought.

He appreciated the warning, but he would do anything he could to help her, and as long as she was hoping to get the inn open, he would help her for free and give her the biggest discount he could on the materials. Even selling them at cost if necessary. He wasn't in it to get rich, but he was definitely into Leiklyn for the rest of his life, if she'd have him.

She seemed like she liked him okay, wasn't close to changing her mind as they talked every day and usually ate lunch together. Sometimes they ate supper together when he didn't need to get back to the store to do necessary things there. Regardless, he spent as much time as he could with her, and she seemed to enjoy it, wanting to spend time with him as well.

Still, the lack of funds had pushed back the opening, and neither one of them had said anything about taking their relationship any further beyond what they'd already discussed.

Maybe he regretted his big words of wanting to take the relationship slow. He for sure wanted to move faster than what they were.

"I guess I'll be seeing you early tomorrow morning," Ethan said to Trent as they walked down to the kitchen together. Leiklyn was having an online video call with her friends about something she'd been pretty excited about at lunchtime but hadn't wanted to go into details about in case it didn't work out.

"It's the Fourth of July. Do you think Mom's really gonna make us work on a holiday?"

"She might not make you work, and she probably wouldn't make me. But I'll be here anyway. Needs to be done."

"Maybe I can sleep in for an hour at least though. I don't mind working, but sometimes getting out of bed is hard."

"I can't disagree with that. I have the same problem. It helps to get to bed earlier, but sometimes that doesn't happen." He nodded his head at the clock on the wall which was showing nine o'clock.

"I know Mom would like it if you stay for supper. I think she's still on her call though."

"I need to get home and do some paperwork for the shop, as much as I love staying and chatting with you guys. I've probably neglected it more than I should have so far this summer."

"I'm gonna eat, shower, and go to bed, in that order," Trent said with a grin as Ethan stuck his head in the dining room and lifted a hand, waving at Leiklyn who smiled and waved back but kept talking.

He didn't bother her but nodded at Trent and told him good night as he walked through the kitchen and out the back door.

It slammed behind him, and he'd taken two steps down the porch before he saw Myla kneeling at the box where Cheddar had her six kittens last week.

Ethan stopped on the step, propping one leg up on the porch and leaning an elbow down on his leg.

"Didn't see you there at first, Myla."

"I'm sorry. I probably startled you." Her tone was subdued and sad.

"The kittens seem to grow almost as you watch them. Every time I look at them, they seem visibly bigger."

"I know. It's pretty amazing. But they're still so helpless."

"They need their mom. That's what moms are for."

"A human baby is even more helpless. At least kittens can get around. Even if they can't see or hear."

"That's true. If a human baby were lying in a box, it wouldn't take long for it to die. But cats don't exactly have arms to pick them up, so God had to do something different with kittens."

Myla smiled a little, and it made him feel good to help the gloomy look disappear from her face. "It is just so amazing how the kittens trust their mom completely to do everything for them. Everything."

"They would die without her for sure," he said.

Leiklyn hadn't exactly shared a whole lot about what was going on with Myla, and he hadn't asked, not only because they really hadn't spent much time together but also figuring that what was private between Myla and her mother wasn't any of his business.

But he could talk to Myla and often did. Normally over lunch with other people around.

"You know I like to think that dads are important, because that's what I'd be, but the fact of the matter is pretty much every baby except a human baby and maybe seahorses would die without his mother."

"Seahorses?" Myla said. There was enough light from the light pole down by the parking area to shed a little glow on her face and see she was smiling. He could hear the humor in her voice too.

"Don't male seahorses carry the babies around or something?" he asked, trying to dig through the information in his head and pull that little tidbit out.

"I don't know. Sounds neat anyway."

"Yeah. Different. They're not mammals though. Most mammals need their moms for food and protection, and if they're to grow up properly, they need their mom's touch and love."

"A big responsibility," she said.

"Sure is."

"I suppose Mom told you that I decided to get an abortion."

She sounded thoughtful, and he thought maybe she'd forgotten who she was talking to, but then maybe because he'd pretty much lived at her house for the last several weeks, eating almost every meal together, maybe she felt comfortable. He wasn't sure, but he answered her anyway.

"She said you weren't sure what you were going to do."

"I know she'll be disappointed in me if I do."

"I don't think that's the biggest reason to not."

Her head snapped up, and he supposed he didn't phrase that sentence very well, because her eyes were narrowed like she couldn't figure out what he was saying. But after a few seconds, they opened back up and she nodded.

"You're right."

She could think he was right all day long and still do what she wanted rather than what she knew she should. So he didn't say anything.

"When I look at these kittens, I think about how innocent they are and how much they need their mom's protection, and it makes me feel like the baby I'm carrying is the same. It's depending on me. And that scares me, a lot actually, but it also makes me feel like...like if I don't keep her safe, who's going to? Like...like there needs to be something more important than me...I feel protective."

"Think that's the mom in you coming out. That's what you're supposed to feel."

"It's seems kind of mean to hurt something that I was meant to protect."

"Yeah, you'd be pretty upset with Cheddar if, instead of taking care of her kittens, she killed them. Or walked away from them. Or didn't care about them."

"I sure would. I'd say she's a terrible mother."

"I guess pretty much everyone would."

"Yeah." Her breath came out long and slow, and then she said, "Thinking about that made me realize that just because something is convenient and legal doesn't make it right. I know I would think of myself as a bad person for a really long time if I do what I said I was going to do."

"I've heard people struggle with it."

Leiklyn said she had told Myla about her abortion, but she hadn't included him.

So he said, "I paid for half of your mother's abortion. That's the single thing I've done in my life that I regret the very most. I'll regret it until I die."

At that, her head snapped up, and her mouth fell open. "You're the guy."

He looked down and nodded. "I am."

"But... But... You seem like such a nice guy."

He had to laugh a little at that. "Just because people seem nice doesn't mean they're good. In fact, I think everybody has a lot of bad in them. We just hide it."

"But I was picturing someone terrible. Someone... I guess Mom never said that the guy was a jerk. Or anything like that. I just made assumptions."

"Sometimes assumptions can get us into trouble. Probably not in that case though. I was young and immature and stupid. All the bad things you're thinking are probably true."

"No. I don't think so."

"Regardless, I'm kind of hoping your mom gives me another chance, and I can be a little smarter about things this time."

"Mom had better give you another chance. You're old, but so is she. Other than that, you're pretty much perfect and Mom deserves a nice guy. I barely know my real dad, but he's selfish... Maybe I shouldn't criticize him, since I was on the verge of making a really selfish decision."

"I think we're all selfish. Something to fight all your life. I suppose it's the people who aren't aware that they're selfish who are the most dangerous."

"Or irritating."

He laughed. "That too."

She tilted her head. "Thanks for listening to me. I had pretty much decided what I wanted to do, but you helped clarify some things for me."

Ethan stood. "Thanks for talking to me. I think that's usually the issue, isn't it?"

"Finding someone who will listen?"

"Yeah."

"You're different than most adults. But so is my mom. None of my friends like their moms, but my mom is the best."

"I guess I can't argue with you about that. God blessed you."

"He has. I just don't know if I can be that good of a mom to my baby."

"Sometimes loving something means giving it up."

"I'm not having an abortion."

"Adoption?"

"Maybe that's my next decision."

"You have a little while to make it."

"It's going slow too."

"I think when you're suffering or uncomfortable, time stands still."

"I know exactly what you mean. And I have to agree with that."

"I'll see you tomorrow, Myla." He started down the steps as she said good night, thankful that Leiklyn had raised such a thoughtful and considerate daughter. Not many teens appreciated what they had in their parents. It was refreshing to see one that did.

Chapter 23

A week later Ethan walked by the front desk on his way up the stairs. He'd gone into town for some more paint and left Trent upstairs painting a bathroom on the fourth room they'd started.

It was almost done.

The bearded man who'd checked into his room four days ago came down the stairs. Leiklyn hadn't said much about him other than he'd booked for more than a month and she just couldn't cancel his reservation, no matter what the financial future of the Inn was.

"Lots of construction going on around here," the man said.

It took Ethan a second to realize the man was talking to him. In the four days he'd been there, he'd pretty much kept to himself.

"Yeah. We're slowly getting it fixed up." He stopped at the bottom of the stairs and waited for the man to descend.

"I'm Drake." The man held out his hand.

"Ethan." Ethan grabbed his hand, realizing as he looked Drake in the eye that he was much younger than Ethan had originally thought – maybe late thirties. He also looked strangely familiar.

"So, I know this is probably a weird request, but before I -" He cut off abruptly like he'd almost said more than he should have. His teeth flashed in the bushy beard, which was when Ethan realized why the dude looked familiar – he was the guy in the billboard advertisement for the latest Hollywood blockbuster.

Ethan wasn't into movies much, but he'd considered asking Leiklyn if her kids and she would like to go see it. He hadn't, just because they'd been working so hard and long on the inn.

Drake coughed as though trying to cover his slip up. "My dad worked construction out on Long Island when I was a kid. I was wondering...would you need some help? I know how to run a hammer and a drill."

"Have you done drywall or flooring?"

152

"Sure. I can plumb pretty well, too, although I'm not great with wiring."

"You're hired."

"I don't want paid. I just want –" Again the man cut off abruptly. "Actually, minimum wage is fine."

Ethan gave the man a shrewd look. He didn't want someone working for him who wasn't going to be honest and upright. Although he would certainly not begrudge the man his privacy.

Deciding the guy was just trying to stay anonymous and there was no harm in that, Ethan said, "That's fine. When do you want to start?"

"Um...now?"

Ethan smiled. "No better time than the present, right?"

"Something like that."

"Come on up. We're cutting it close with supplies, but you can have your pick of the jobs we've got going on. Although I do have to say, if it's going to bother you that a fourteen year old has seniority over you, you might want to find a different job."

"I can be the supporting actor. Um, handyman."

Ethan bit back a grin and started up the stairs.

Drake was as good as his word, and Ethan didn't need to supervise him long to know the man was just as good as he was at plumbing, if not better.

Leiklyn seemed tired and preoccupied and almost depressed and she said she was going to bed as soon as they were done eating, but as had become their custom, he'd arrived before daylight and met her on the rise overlooking the lake.

She didn't say anything as he walked over, but he took her hand, lacing his fingers with hers and loving how they fit together. No matter how tired or despondent he was, being hand-in-hand with Leiklyn always lifted his spirits.

"I have ten dollars left in my account," she said. Her voice was small and forlorn.

"I have a little bit more left in mine," he said, not wanting to make fun of her problems, but feeling like if they ran out of money and couldn't finish fixing up the inn, it wouldn't be the end of the world as long as they were still together.

"When I talked to Willan and Tiffany last week, Tiffany thought her ex was going to have to cough up the money, but, it turns out, the judge ruled in his favor and she's getting nothing." She sighed and turned to him, deep sadness in her eyes. "I was really counting on that to pull us through. We just don't have enough rooms open to make a go of it yet."

"I know."

"I've been offered a job at a company where a friend and coworker of mine from my previous job was hired. She put in a great recommendation for me. The company interviewed me two days ago and the job offer was in my inbox this morning."

"Congratulations!" he said, trying to put enthusiasm into his voice while his heart dove to the ground and shriveled there. "Is the job close by?" he asked, hoping, hoping it was. How was he supposed to be happy if Leiklyn were moving to, say, New York?

"No. It's in Oklahoma."

He swallowed, his fingers tightening around hers like that could keep her from going.

"Are you going to take it?"

There was a long pause, the mist slowly moving across the beach, shifting, showing the sand before hiding it again. Finally she said, "I don't have a choice." She put a hand on his arm. "You understand that, right? I would stay. I want to stay. Even if I don't have the inn, the last thing I want to do is move away from you and whatever it is that we're rebuilding. I want this. You. You're the best thing that's ever happened to me and I want with all my heart and soul to hold on to you. But…"

She swallowed, loud in the predawn stillness. "But I have to take care of my family. I have to support my kids, and Myla…"

"She's chosen to have the baby?"

"Yes. She's very adamant about it. But, she's thinking about giving it up for adoption."

"That's hard. But smart, I think."

"It's going to work out, I'm sure. But we need health insurance. Mine runs out at the end of next month. This job would solve that problem, too."

"Marry me. Stay. The hardware store won't make us rich, but we'd be together."

"I can't do that. You've already given me more than you should have. I can't be a leech that keeps sucking the life out of you."

"You give me life!"

Her eyes held sadness as she gazed up at him. "It's not just me. I come with two kids. The apartment above the hardware store is one bedroom, right?"

"We can live at the inn."

Her brows went up like she hadn't thought of that.

"I know having an empty bank account is scary. I get it. But we can make it work. I...I've been falling in love with you all over again. I'm there. I...I love you." Why were the words so scary? "I'm not thinking it will be easy, but I am thinking we can do it together." He put his hand on her arm, sliding it down until he clasped both of hers in his. "Please don't walk away from me again."

He closed his mouth, unwilling to beg more than he already had. If she wanted him, she'd stay. Money wouldn't matter. Neither would where they lived or what they did for a living.

"I made that mistake the first time, didn't I?"

"Yeah. You did. I didn't speak up then and ask you for more. To stay. To take a chance on me. But I'm asking you now."

"You were serious about getting married?"

"Yes. I wish I'd been prepared. You deserve a better proposal than that."

"No. I don't deserve better. I'm getting you. How could anything be better than that?"

"You'll give me a big head."

"Hardly," she smiled, and her smile gave him hope that, while she was disappointed about the inn, she could see a future with both of them together.

"Did you really want that job?" he asked, moving closer and putting his arms around her. "We don't have to stay here if you want to go to Oklahoma. I can sell out and find something there."

He didn't want to leave Blueberry Beach, but for Leiklyn, he would.

"No. I just didn't see any other way."

He put a hand on her cheek, brushing lightly over its cool softness before moving it around behind her head. "I wish I would have gone after you. My biggest regret is losing our baby and the next biggest is letting you go."

"Let's forget about regrets and make new, beautiful memories."

"You have the best ideas," he murmured, lowering his head and touching his lips with hers. New, yet familiar, their kiss was filled with hope for the future and sweet passion that had always flared so easily between them.

When he finally lifted his head and opened his eyes, the darkness had faded, although the mist had turned the entire world white, enclosing them in a flowing curtain of their own private world.

"You are incredible." His words came out laden with emotion, his cheek brushing hers, his mouth next to her ear.

"That was so much better than I remember," she whispered back

"How soon would you like to get married?" he asked.

"Today?" The smile in her voice was clear, but there was an underlying longing that turned his lips up in pleasure.

"I'm good with that."

"I want to tell the kids first. I know they'll be okay with it. They both love you, but I want them to feel included."

"Me too." He couldn't agree more and loved that her children were a priority for her.

"Maybe we could do a little more kissing, first?" she asked, turning her head and brushing her lips along his jaw.

"I think I might have mentioned how good your ideas are. And that one's one of your best." He lowered his head and kissed the woman he loved in the misty morning.

Epilogue

Willan Hawkins walked up the steps of the Indigo Inn.

One of her two best friends was getting married tomorrow and Willan had not gotten her a wedding gift, but she was bringing something better – money to continue fixing up the inn.

Her Aunt Tabitha had passed away two weeks ago. While Willan wasn't super close to her dear aunt, she was the only family the older woman still spoke with.

And she was the only one mentioned in the will.

Willan had attended the funeral – the preacher, his brother and a stray dog (which quickly got chased out of the church) had been the only attendees.

Still, it was the least she could do since the lady had left her the entirety of her considerable estate.

Also, the dog had still been hanging around the corner of the church when Willan walked out, after saying a heartfelt "thank you" to the corpse in the casket, so she figured she could be generous, and also figured she was going to be turning over a new leaf. No more perfection in her life. She was going to become friends with dirt and mess and even take a risk or two. Maybe.

She opened the front door and walked in. Probably she should have been watching where she was going rather than thinking about how she was going to change her life. If she had been, maybe she wouldn't have kicked over the bucket of paint that was sitting in the middle of the floor.

"Watch what you're doing, lady!" A bearded man wearing coveralls and a ball cap exclaimed in a voice that was definitely angry, if not loud.

"Any idiot knows you don't set a paint can in the middle of the floor!"

"I was moving the ladder. There isn't any place else to set it!" The man's voice contained a growl that she might have called sexy if his anger had been directed at someone else. "There's going to be a wedding here tomorrow and you've just ruined the floor!"

"I would say you ruined it just as much as I did, since you set the paint there." She narrowed her eyes, unaccountably angry at getting yelled at by the hired help. "Regardless, it's your job to get it cleaned up and have this floor looking perfect. Leiklyn deserved the best wedding day ever."

"You spilt it. You clean it up." The man hissed.

"You're the hired help. I own this inn. You clean it up." Willan said, then turned, without giving him a chance to answer and stormed down the hall toward the kitchen. Normally she would have apologized and helped clean it up, but the man had been unkind and mean.

Or maybe she was the one who had been unkind and mean.

Wasn't that her problem? She always blamed everything on everyone else. Or on something else. She never took responsibility for her actions and reached out for what she wanted.

She was done playing the victim. She was also done being the perfect princess. Her steps slowed, then stopped.

If she wanted to change, she had to stop thinking about it, and just do it.

Swallowing her pride, she turned, determined she would apologize and clean up the mess herself, although she had no idea how to get paint off tile. The rest of her life started today, and it was going to be a lot different from here on out.

~~~

Thanks so much for reading! If you'd like to read Willen's story, you can get it HERE[1].

If you'd like to interact with me join my Facebook group[2].

---

1. https://www.amazon.com/gp/product/B099BVRTHV

2.   https://www.facebook.com/groups/jessiegussman

I'd love for you to sign up for my newsletter[3] to read stories about my daily life on the farm, get deals on my books and occasionally get other sweet romance deals as well.

---

3.   https://dl.bookfunnel.com/97elto4gwl

Made in the USA
Columbia, SC
06 February 2023

11879424R00091